Henry H. Woodward

Lyrics of the Umpqua

Henry H. Woodward

Lyrics of the Umpqua

ISBN/EAN: 9783744782838

Printed in Europe, USA, Canada, Australia, Japan

Cover: Foto ©Andreas Hilbeck / pixelio.de

More available books at **www.hansebooks.com**

LYRICS OF THE

UMPQUA

BY

HENRY H. WOODWARD

———

NEW YORK
JOHN B. ALDEN, PUBLISHER
1889

CONTENTS.

To Columbia, - - - - - - - 1
The Wandering Boy. A Tale of Two Scouts, - - 2
Beseeching God for Guidance, - - - - 4
Paraphrase of Psalm XII., - - - - - 5
To My Friend Geo. Dove, Esq., - - - - 6
Bryant, - - - - - - - 7
A True Home, - - - - - - 7
The Dying Child, - - - - - - 8
Israelitish Acrostic, - - - - - 10
Psalm XXXV. A Paraphrase, - - - 10
Song, - - - - - - - 13
Reliance on God's Promise, - - - - 14
An Appeal to God, - - - - - 15
Mutations of the Earth's Surface, - - - 16
Mount Etna. An Ode, - - - - - 18
Apostrophe to the Ocean, - - - - 21
The Song of the Modern Sewing-girl. Tune, Washing Day, 27
Woman's Love, - - - - - - 28
Lines Written on the Death of Two Children of a Friend, 29
Ode to Solomon's Song, - - - - 30
Acrostic, - - - - - - 31
The Gilded Dome, - - - - - 31
The Cotter's Home. A Contrast, - - - 33
Lines Addressed to Capt. W. W. Kiddle, Late of the White
        Star Line Steamer "Celtic," - - - 36
Sea Song, - - - - - - 37
Creation the Work of God, - - - - 38
Lines Written in a Lady's Album, - - - 40
Dulce et Decorum est pro Patria Mori, - - 41

Unseen Power. An Apostrophe,   42
Ode on Contentment,   46
Idyllic Ode,   47
Contemplation. An Indian's Soliloquy,   49
Ode. Jealousy,   51
The Village Band,   52
De Mortuis Nil Nisi Bonum,   54
The Precepts of the Holy Law,   56
Acrostic,   57
The Advantages of a Country Life,   58
The Libertine,   61
Memorial Ode,   64
To Indian War Veterans,   66
The Veteran's Reply,   67
The Divinity of Nature,   68
In Memoriam,   71
The Lilies of the Field,   73
Ode. The Pioneers of the N. W. Coast,   74
To the Rainbow,   77
Address to the Deity,   77
Ode to Jerusalem,   78
The Recording of the Oral Law,   79
Song. Israelitish,   80
An Eulogy,   81
Conquiescat in Pace,   82
The Departed Year,   83
Song,   84
Acrostic. Marriage,   85
The Homeless Girl,   85
A Panegyric,   87
Ode. On the Admission of California,   89
To Roseburgh, Oregon,   90
In Memoriam,   92
Lines,   93
Requiescat in Pace,   94
Acrostic,   95
Martial Music,   96

The Rescue,   · · · · · · · 98
Zeuxia. A Picture with a Moral,   · · · 100
Episodes of the Mariner's Life,   · · · · 102
An Epopee. Life on the Frontier,   · · · 106
Songs,   · · · · · · · 108
On Death. A Soliloquy,   · · · · 109
Lines Addressed to William Wake, Esq.,   · · · 110
Low Ash,   · · · · · · · 111
Bible Blessings,   · · · · · · 112
Song,   · · · · · · · 113
Happiness,   · · · · · · · 114
A Reverie,   · · · · · · 115
Reason versus Bigotry,   · · · · 115
Hindoo Mythology,   · · · · · 119
Hymns,   · · · · · · 121-191

LYRICS OF THE UMPQUA.

TO COLUMBIA.

HAIL to thee, Freedom's great resting-place,
Harbor of sweet refuge for men of every race!
Thou knowest no color, thou askest not man's creed,
And the oppress'd thou ever help'st in need.
Descendants of an heroic race now till thy richly soil,
And who of that right them ever dare despoil?
From every point thy standard high is reared,
'Tis lov'd by thy true sons, and by all despots feared.
They fear the example thou hast set to man,
For by intelligence he can a *document* plan
Whereby his right to property, liberty and life
Can be to him secured, defying autocratic strife.
Thy friends in foreign lands respect thy goodly name,
Especially in yonder isle from whence the Pilgrims
     came.
So hail to thee, proud child of nation's mother so dear,
Thrice hail to thee, fair land, a land without a peer!

THE WANDERING BOY.

(A TALE OF TWO SCOUTS.)

BEFORE the morning's sun had brightly shone,
Two scouts from the whites' encampment rose
To search for the route the redmen had gone ;
They were armed cap-à-pie for deadly foes.
The twain ranged o'er rough mountain's side,
And peered o'er precipices' craggy steep ;
Into rocky cañons they closely spied
Where foaming cataracts high did leap ;
They mark'd tracks on a dim Indian trail,
Yet they saw no grim warriors near.
At last the foot-prints began to fail,
When in dense woods they silently steer.
At last they saw a dim-like form
Swiftly running thro' the underbrush.
They made ready their guns for ambush storm,
And darting forward made a rush.
Soon the quarry was brought to bay,
When lo ! behold, 'twas an Indian boy
Who had been roaming many a day.
He was dejected, in tatter'd rags, and coy.
He trembled with fear like an aspen leaf,
And pearly tears fell thick and fast ;
They ask'd him where was his chief,

When towards the cañon his eyes he cast.
He'd escaped away from friends afar
One misty morn, at break of day,
When the whites and Indians were at war,
From camp (but where he would not say).
They cheered him as best they knew that morn.
His form was bony, weak and gaunt,
Of food his budget was entirely shorn,
And his tender bosom with grief did pant.
The scouts, in his own language, said
That they intended him no harm ;
The feeble boy lifted his drooping head,
And soon did vanish his dire alarm.
They took him gently by the hand,
And fed him well with nourishing food,
Yet still he'd sigh for his native land
Away yonder, near the merry greenwood.
Anon they took him o'er mount and dale,
To "Umpqua's" hospitable land,
And there to the "Agent" told this tale,
"That the boy had wandered from the band.

BESEECHING GOD FOR GUIDANCE.

LORD, keep me from superstitious fear,
That dread of harm when none is near;
It often lurks in the mind of sinful man;
O let me the gulf of darkness span.
Enrich my mind with sacred things of light,
So that my actions may be guided right;
Inspire me with counsel from thy throne,
And elevate my soul to a higher zone;
Let not vain thoughts ever o'er me steal,
But my wounded spirit do thou heal;
Awake or sleeping in Thee I e'er confide,
Throughout my life a due course to guide.
I pray root out the vain desires I crave,
That I ne'er become dark passion's slave;
Give me force of will my anger to control,
And keep invidious envy from my soul;
Steer me from false pride's domineering way,
So that covetous cravings can ne'er gain sway;
Instil into my heart the course I need
To keep me from avarice and sordid greed;
Grant me fortitude against adversity dread,
To meet it with firm heart, also with a clear head,
And ever look to Thee when occur changes new,
And at thy foot-stool for every favor sue.

By rectitude of conduct may I find friends !
On such our worldly happiness depends ;
Let no spiteful malice occupy my mind's domain,
And the demon of jealousy fetter with an iron chain.
O let my spirit feel Thou art ever near
To shield me from difficulties round me here !
Guide Thou my thoughts beyond the things of sense,
And for friendly kindness I should give recompense.
Then, when my mortal coil of life is run,
Let my spirit rest beyond the sun !

PARAPHRASE OF PSALM XII.

Help, Lord ! the godly man ceaseth who lov'd Thee, to
    adore,
The faithful fail among thy children sore ;
Every one with his neighbor doth vanity speak,
With flattering lips and double heart they sneak.
The Lord shall cut off all lips that flatter.
And the tongue that speaketh proudly matter.
Who have said "With our tongue we will prevail ;
Our lips are our own—who is lord o'er this vale ? "
" For the oppression of the poor, for the sighing of the
    needy,
Now will I arise," saith the Lord, "right speedy."

The Lord's words are pure as the silver tried
In a furnace of earth, **seven** times purified,
Thou shalt keep them, and shalt them hoard
From this generation forever, O Lord!
On every side the wicked walk,
When the vilest men exalted stalk.

TO MY FRIEND GEO. DOVE, ESQ.

OLD friend, this day I truly write
   A few lines of my friendly feeling;
'Tis many years since I did thee sight,
   Yet in my vision **thy form is** stealing.

May you happy be is my sincere hope
   (I know you are good, also kind and true);
Tho' I'm on Pacific's far-off slope,
   Thy heart to me is clear as morning's **drop of dew,**

Thy firm friendship to me I'll ne'er forget
   While life lasts in this mortal frame,
Tho' we're both nearing to life's sunset,
   Yet I'll cherish and remember thy good name.

Thou wert loved and honored in the *Bark*,
   And thy name is symbolic of Peace and Love;
Should my future life be either bright or dark,
   I shall ever think of thee as—friend "George Dove."

BRYANT.

PATRIARCH of poesy, thy voice is heard no more,
    Friends whom thow didst love now sigh in vain,
For thou art singing on a happier shore,
    Thy sacred songs in a heavenly strain.
Thou hast left us "Thanatopsis," and there we find
Samples of thy goodness and genius of mind.
No praise thou need'st from humble pen of man,
    No bubble of fame can stir a vein of pride ;
Thou lived'st long past the Script's indited span,
    And trusted to thy God to be thy saving guide.
And "where rolls the Oregon that hears no sound
Save its own dashing," thy inspired tomes are found.

A TRUE HOME.

O MAN, where is thy truest home ?
    The place which thou lovest best ?
Wherever thou dost choose to roam
    Thy heart that love will test.

'Tis not alone the place of birth
    Thy lasting home can surely be ;
The countries of the sea and earth
    Are thine to wand'ring see.

Wherever thou rest thy weary head,
   And where'er thy steps are free,
In whatever land thou hast sped,
   'Tis but transient home for thee.

If thou in frigid zones dost stray,
   Or to tropics' sun-lit clime,
There thou canst pass each dreary day,
   At the shrine of old dull Time.

Thy real home is where heart-strings cling,
   The goal to which thou'lt fondly steer.
No matter how charming strange voices sing,
   Nature sighs for sweeter tones to hear.

THE DYING CHILD.

HE lay upon his bed of pain
   For many a weary day,
Stricken by fever's parching bane,
   When these words the child did say:

'Bring me my purse and I'll give,
   To brothers and sisters dear ;
A part of my hoard shall freely go
   Their spirits now to cheer.

And you, dear father, the rest take
  In memory of your son ;
My cards I'll give for a keepsake
  To my play-mates every one."

In piteous accents he exclaimed,
  "Dear Pa, I don't wish to die."
The pillows were laid as his will framed,
  With many a parental sigh.

"Dear Pa !" he said, "I can't speak more !
  And in torment tossed about,
When his spirit flew to Jordan's shore,
  God's angels showing the route,

Weep not for him—his suffering's o'er
  Awhile God gave him to parents' keeping ;
Now his soul is on a happy shore,
  While in earth his body is sleeping.

ISRAELITISH ACROSTIC.

Note now Bereschith, in Genesis 'tis found
On that the diction of this theme will sound.
The words Bara, Rakia, Arez and Schamaim,
And when interpreted meaneth, "Tehomoth, I am,"
Rightly signifying God made earth below and sky
    above,
In fact also that the heavens and sea are tokens of His
    love. ·

Composed of words in Hebrew language of old,
On their hope of Heaven to Aglar the chosen hold;
Now this acrostic will the Notaricon unfold.

    Note.—Aglar signifies a drop of dew — an emblem of God.

PSALM XXXV.

(A PARAPHRASE.)

Plead my *cause*, O Lord, with them that cause me strife,
Fight against them that fight with me for life !
Take shield and buckler, and for mine help Thou stand;
Draw out the spear, and stop persecution in the land.
Say unto my soul, "I'm thy salvation ;" confound and
    shame them that it seek;
Turn back and confuse them that devise against the
    weak ;

Let them be as chaff before the wind, and let thy angel
    give them chase ;
Let their way be dark and slippery, and let thy angel
    their works deface.
For without cause have they hid their net in a pit,
Which without cause they dug, therein my soul to fit.
Let destruction come upon him at unawares,
And let the net catch him in its snares ;
Into that very destruction let him fall,
And joyful in the Lord shall be my soul.
Glad by salvation my bones shall say, "Lord, who's
    like Thee, that shields the poor
From him that is too strong ? yea, and furthermore,
The poor and needy that he spoileth him.
False witnesses rose and laid charges that to me were
    dim,
They rewarded me evil for good to the spoiling of my
    soul.
But as for me, when they were sick, in sackcloth I did
    toil,
I humbled my soul with fasting, and my prayer to my
    bosom return'd ;
I behaved as if he'd been friend or brother, and as if
    for my mother I mourn'd.
But in my adversity they rejoiced, and gathered them-
    selves together ;

Yea, the abjects gathered themselves together (naught
    could them sever),
They tore me unceasingly; deceitful mockers in feasts
    their teeth gnash.
Lord, how long wilt Thou look on ! Rescue me from
    destruction's gash,
And my darling from the lions, and I will thanks give,
In the great congregation I will praise Thee where the
    people live.
Let not my enemies wrongfully rejoice over me,
Nor let them wink with the eye with hateful decree.
Without cause they speak not peace, but devise
Deceitful matters ; 'gainst the quiet of the land arise ;
Yea they opened their mouth wide against me,
And said : "Aha ! aha ! our eye did see !"
This Thou hast seen, O Lord, keep not silence !
O Lord, be not far from me ! stir from hence,
And awake to my judgment even to my cause,
My God and my Lord ; judge me by thy laws,
O Lord my God, according to thy righteousness,
And let them not rejoice over my distress.   .
Let them not say, "We would have it so,"
Let them not say, " He's swallowed up in woe !"
Shamed and confused be they that at my hurt rejoice,
Shamed and dishonor'd that magnify themselves with
    boasting voice !

Let them shout for joy and be glad that favor my
    righteous cause,
Yea, continually say, "the Lord be praised, for his
    servant prosperity knows !"
And I'll speak of thy righteousness with my tongue,
And of thy good praises all the day long.

SONG.

If thy country should need thee, O never say "No,"
But be thou the first one to strike the hard blow,
Right onward to march, at the front take thy stand,
And be thou ever ready to defend thy good land.

Though dangers beset thee in front and in rear,
Do thou never flinch, or be nervous with fear ;
But stand like a hero in the struggle and woe,
And hurl to the ground the dastardly foe.

Ne'er be daunted, perchance, if the column e'er quail,
But let thy blows be dealt as fast as sharp hail ;
When ordered to thy post, be sure to rally around ;
Though thy comrades fall thick, still stand to thy ground.

Thou hast bade adieu to the loved ones at home,
And through the **campaign** must forage and roam ;
If stinted in rations let thy spirit **ne'er** droop,
But set an **example** to the rest of the troop.

What if **bullets** rattle round thee in the hostile affray ?
Remember **thy** bullets in foemen's ranks stray ;
They're in just as much danger as thy comrades in rank,
And **lots of your** foes have to the crimson'd ground sank.

When the war is **all over, and** thy duty is done,
Thy mother at home will be proud **of her** son.
If thou shouldst be wounded, or crippled for life,
Thy country will reward thee as a hero in the strife.

RELIANCE ON GOD'S PROMISE.

I SIGH not for power, I crave not for wealth,
I live for God's pleasure, who granteth me health ;
I search His good **word** for wisdom on high,
And to keep a clear conscience is all I e'er sigh.

What is power on earth but others' troubles to share ?
What is gold to inherit but cankering care ?
But the words of Jehovah are pure silver tried,
In fiery furnace, and seven times purified.

A clear mind and pure **heart are** blessings to last,
That no deep **disappointment** can e'er overcast.
Pangs of **sorrow may** ensue—'tis allotted to man
Aye! even **hard** chastenings **may** be the Lord's plan.

Yet He has promised He'll not always chastise,
But will give all a chance for the Heavenly prize.
I pray most devoutly He will pardon us all,
And **in mercy** will sound the trumpet's last call.

AN APPEAL TO GOD.*

IF my spirit is a divine spark,
 As the *Hindoos* would have us **believe,**
O Lord, wouldst Thou in mercy hark
 To this prayer, **and mine** receive!

And may my spirit soul e'er be
 Acceptable to Thy loving sight;
May I ne'er cease to ask of Thee
 To keep my wand'ring spirit right.

* The Hindoos believe that the spirit of man is a *spark of God,*

MUTATIONS OF THE EARTH'S SURFACE.

Where we abide, once dashed the wave,
And many a tremendous storm passed o'er;
On other continents the sea did lave,
And we cannot trace the lines of shore.
Ages have passed, and great changes been wrought
By nature's convulsive heaves and throes;
Diligently intellectual men have sought
Her strange freaks and inexplicable laws.
Actions of past periods by scientists are seen;
Intricate problems are solved by learned care;
It is ascertained the ocean's waves have been
Where now the Lion makes his bone-strewed lair.
And where'er an antiquarian's penetrating mind
Searches where archæologists have excavated,
Many marvellous works he will often find,
And then new theories are surely ventilated.
Mountains now stand where plains once stood;
Plains now stand where mounts have soar'd;
Pinks now grow where once stood greenwood,
And woods grow where flowers once perfume pour'd.
How came these changes in long ages past,
When reptiles now extinct once crawl'd around?
And will these primitive changes be the last?
Or will mighty earthquakes upheave the ground?

We know not what the future change may be
Of this mutable and fickle-crusted sphere ;
But by land delving and dredging in the sea,
Man can reason by analogy whilst he's here.
Alas ! human thought but transiently lives ;
For man's life is but a brief-like span,
'Tis a feeble link man's knowledge e'er gives
To cause and effect of God's worldly plan.
Intense heat the earth's deep centre holds,
'Tis a roaring furnace—a sulphuric fire,
With watery crevices held in rocky moulds
Which burst, and vapor makes old "Etna's" ire.
Even zones of climate have often changed,
And where tropical plants now grow so grand,
The huge glaciers have crushingly ranged,
And rigorous winters have ruled the land.
Reversely, where the ice-king now reigns supreme,
In zones spread o'er with everlasting snow,
Once the flora of the tropics did fragrantly teem,
And old Sol was king with fierce burning glow.
Great mastodons' bones are found in remote places,
Many deeply and to the north of tropical line.
Oft a keen scientist the hidden mystery traces
By scrutinizing the geological mine.
How wonderful thy works, O Lord in heaven,
Which Thou hast done on this mundane sphere !

Internal fiery vaults when by Thee riven,
Deal destruction, showing Thou art near.
Mundane upheavals are then Thy holy will,
Incomprehensible changes Thou didst perform ;
Sometimes external thunders are calmly still,
When again they burst forth in terrific storm.
Who will solve the phenomena of nature ?
What era will bring these changes to light ?
What will be the curious nomenclature,
To set future antiquarians aright ?
The present theories are fitful as the wind,
Philosophers have vented ideas, alas ! to fall,
And Nature's various moods are hard to find ;
They're only known to One, the Maker of them all.

MOUNT ETNA.

AN ODE.

O'er Etna's crater'd mount the seething lava flowed,
Down to the fated city the molten debris ran,
'Twas then calamitous woes were sowed
That appalled the heart of stricken man.
Thunder tones of the monster echoed o'er the vale,
And glittering sparks flew o'er the rippling wave,
'Midst the tumult sounded the heart-rent wail
Of lonely woman and Sicily's son so brave,

At night, too, in grandeur the convulsions were sublime,
As from the cauldron in fitful throbs was forced the fire,
Lava engulfing the innocent, also the men of crime,
As to lofty heights the lurid sparks mount higher.
Devastation mark'd the spot where'er the lava ran,
Despair was pictured in every human face ;
Now, with saddened feelings, modern tourists scan
The site of a once proud city whose wreck they trace.
All nations flock to the scene of dread eruptive mount,
And round the beach in reverent awe they stand,
In mood reflecting on Nature's wondrous fount,
Impressed that 'tis the work of a Mighty Hand.
Ah ! who can tell how soon convulsed our site may be,
And its present state of pleasing surface suddenly
      change,
And like fiery Etna cause men in terror quick to flee
From rushing lava of some new mount's crater'd range?
In the twinkle of an eye the throbs of nature come,
Perhaps at a time when men hilarious are and gay ;
The pulsation shakes the fabric of the mighty dome,
When *Nature* is the conqueror, and *men's* works pass
      away.
We can point to "Salvador," where volcanic mount
      arose
'Midst richly plain where coffee-planters lovely homes
      had made ;

Suddenly its towering form burst forth by nature's
      throes,
Sending flashes of flame in brilliant colors array'd.
The running fiery lava that fair land once curs'd,
And terrified the heart of unsuspecting man,
As loud explosions from the strange mount burst,
And some from the scene of destruction horrified ran.
Upward flew the fiery meteors in airy space;
The atmosphere around with dense smoke was filled,
And men's domiciles were engulf'd at the monster's base;
Where once in peace the happy folks their vineyards
      tilled.
The roaring, deafening noise was heard in lands afar;
Sulphurous was the scented air, tho' grand was the
      mount to view,
And the country made desolate by internal forces at
      war,
When a new-created mount from their *antagonisms*
      grew.
Such is the pictured theme of one of Nature's freaks
That, alas! too true occurred (not a century ago).
For when gaseous forces war, nature for them an out-
      let seeks,
Which oft to man entaileth misery and woe.
In places unsuspected by man she bursts an opening
      out

For the elements that are within the earth to vent their
    wrath ;
In consternation the wretched people loudly shout,
Calling on their God to lead them to His saving path.
It seemed as though a branch of infernal regions had
    come
To show man the destined end of this terrestrial world,
So that he could turn his thoughts to that Heavenly
    home
"Not made with hands," and where no volcanio
    mounts are hurl'd.

APOSTROPHE TO THE OCEAN.

DEEP and expansive sea, which encircleth
This terrestrial sphere—sublimely
Grand and beautiful in calmly mood,
Like an infant in placid slumber dreaming ;
But awful in thine anger when aroused
By "Boreas" when he disturbs thy peace !
For like unto the passions of mankind
When driven furious to a high degree,
Thou art terrible ; and in agitated mood
Art as an evil spectre to the mariner
Who rides o'er thy billowy convex'd form
When the gale of thy sudden unrest

Dashes his bark from human sight
Into thy immeasurable depth of space,
Which clothes with death—thy nautical embrace,—
And man's resistance is all in vain.

Thou rulest thy realm by a set or laws
By nature framed more inflexible in action
Than mortal despots are on the land.
Thou hast the sterling justice, no distinction
E'er to make between peer or peasant;
Their fates are equally dispensed in trials
Of skill with thee ; as Neptune with his trident
Rides on thy waves triumphantly.
In thy tempests thou takest from mankind
The fruits of their ingenuity and craft
That were framed by their minds and will,
Dashing into fragments the labor of years.
But in thy silent mood thou reflectest
The rays of the lustrous mid-day's sun,
When thy mirrored face becometh
An oceanic paradise where angels
Might serenely and securely dwell.

Thy tides and surges ensnare the rich
And poor alike, as prey caught in the
Fisherman's net.   Perchance some wretched

Being in the swimming struggle might escape
From thy Octopus-like grasp, and outlive
The doom thou hadst in store, and pass
Through the rolling surf whose roar is to many
Of thy victims their dismal funeral dirge.
Oft' thy dashing surges combat the peaceful shore,
And by force and tidal persistence pierce
Asunder the hard granite rock from its
Bed of long ages past, where inert it laid.
And thou aggressively changest the form
Of shore line, which was formed by aid
Of *Time*, old Nature's rule.   Thy encroachments
Were made by the mad Storm King
Undermining the foundation of terra-firma.
Lo ! he conquers and usurps new realms,
And o'er extended domain thy wielded
Sceptre is sustained by his terrific might.
When convulsed thou art wonderful to man,
And when calm art beautiful to his view !
Yet all thy attributes are as antagonisms
In their fitful changes in thy varied moods.
And thou hast a Queen whom thou must obey
As tho' thou wert slave to her despotic will ;
For the moon at seasons rules thee with
Her attractive power, and thou art spell-bound,
Like the deadly cobra, when he is charmed

By subtle influence in India's sunny lands.
Thou lavest around yon fair Island whose spicy
Breezes waft gently seaward to thy vast realm,
Refreshing the weary mariner in equatorial clime,
Or lulling him to balmy sleep.
Thou girtest innumerable isles that are dotted
In thy midst, as marks of love the Creator
Hath set to cheer the mariners on their stormy course.
Thou art the watchful monarch of them all,
Encompassing them with thy love, or storms their
　　　　shores sweeping,
And thy mandates can of existence them deprive.
On thy bosom sails the messenger of peace;
White and spotless are its wings aloft, bearing
Brave and faithful souls.
Grand is such picture, naught in nature or art
Can excel.   She glides majestic, as tho'
Endowed with life like a creature of God.
Controlled is she by them who are bound to thee
By ties of admiration and deep skill, who all
Thy elements of wrath survey in the calm spirit of
Hope for their subsidence ; for they counteract
By daring skill the surges hurl'd by thee,
As if in mockery thou wouldst test
Their firmness against thy crushing force.
There go the huge monsters of destruction from

Their fair havens, to invade and make havoc
With their foes in bloody strife for victory.
Man makes on thee a place of battle for his
Lust of power; then the creatures that are
For thee, and those that dwell on thy bosom,
Flee away in terror at the tumultuous roar of
Their artillery, that were wont to fearlessly follow
In the wake of dove-like peace.
Thou art dyed crimson with the blood
Of the brave who fell, and who have bounded
O'er thee in admiration, love and joy, but whose
Life-blood mingles with thy briny waves to be
Evaporated by sun's rays, and to be again
Diffused where his Creator willeth.
Thou art an aqueous tomb for the proud
And vain. Sometimes acting as their "Nemesis," thou
　　　hurlest
Them to sudden death, and not even a lisped
Prayer is heard by God above when their spirits depart.
They go where none can place a stone to mark
The site of their turbulent ever-shifting grave.
No lofty columns on thy expanse are reared
To eulogize the potentates held in thy grasp,
And the humble mariner's weather-beaten body
Can sleep as calm, and whose loss is mourned as
　　　deeply

Where the sea-birds make their wavy homes
As the highest and proudest in God's realm.
In thy depths are the warrior and the sage,
And thou holdest the aged and the young ;
Aye, even the grave and gay, also the maiden
In her fullness of nature's charms, are swept
Into the vortex thou hast made for their
Reception in thy gloomy moods.   And friends
Do mourn at their losses *here on earth*.
Alas, they mourn in vain.   Thy vast region
Holds their mortal bodies in its embrace,
But not *forever*, and the affectionate can find
Consolation in Holy Writ, indisputable, for therein
Is inscribed, that thou must release thy captives
Who have been swayed to and fro in deep recesses ;
For at the Great Judge's appointed time, when
He issues His decree, "The sea shall give up the
dead,"
Then the spirits that are now weeping and
Have wept their sorrowful tears for the lov'd ones
Thou hast held for ages, shall see the
Resurrected ones as angels in a celestial sphere,
Forever to rest in peace with God, who will,
No doubt, decree that thou shalt never more be
A sepulchre for man who is "made in His own
image."

THE SONG OF THE MODERN SEWING-GIRL.

TUNE—WASHING DAY.

I STITCH, stitch, stitch, stitch, stitch, stitch away,
For now there is some comfort, free from any delay.
The *bastings* and the *gores* are stitched quite complete,
And sewing has now become quite a little treat.

> CHORUS—I stitch, stitch, stitch, stitch, stitch, stitch
> away,
> For this machine was invented to bring
> our muscles into play.

God bless old Howe, the inventor of this worthy ma-
chine !
For it is the *No Plus Ultra*—for good sewing I mean.
So I tread, tread, tread, tread, tread, tread away ;
This is a boon to womankind, every one does say.

> CHORUS—I stitch, stitch, stitch, stitch, stitch, stitch
> away,
> For this machine was invented to bring
> , our muscles into play.

Flounces can be double stitched on *petticoats* of satin,
And embroidered tapestry worked in either Greek or
Latin.
But I would rather stitch the dress to make my bridal
tour,
To please the one I love so dear and sigh for evermore.

Chorus—I stitch, stitch, stitch, stitch, stitch, stitch
away,
For this machine was invented to bring
our muscles into play.

This world is nothing but fine stitches made by our
Master's hand ;
The seas and trees and other things He stitched closely
to the land,
But it's when two hearts are stitched together in *gathering*
close embrace,
Then the work of the *Greatest Inventor* we in love delight
to trace.

Chorus—I stitch, stitch, stitch, stitch, stitch, stitch
away,
For this machine was invented to bring
our muscles into play.

———

WOMAN'S LOVE.

Tell me not that woman's love
Is fickle as the wind,
In truth she's gentle as the dove,
Affectionate and kind.

Tell me not she's artful, vain
Of charms that nature gave her ;
Her heart is free from falsehood's stain,
And her love doth never waver.
Tell me not when age onward creeps
Her love will vanish surely,—
Ah ! woman's fond love never sleeps,
When once she loves—'tis purely.

LINES WRITTEN ON THE DEATH OF TWO CHILDREN OF A FRIEND.

The cherubs died whom our Father gave,
And sad friends are mourning now ;
They sleep together in one small grave,
And we in peace must bow.
How mysterious are the Lord's ways !
For He alone can tell
When He should our spirits raise,
Or make us ill or well.
The Lord gave, and has took away
The two darlings of the heart,
And placed them in a grand array,
To play a heavenly part.

ODE TO SOLOMON'S SONG.

WHEN Solomon wrote his song of praise,
And singers sat in the house of the Lord,
The people of Jerusalem stood in amaze
As they listened to each inspired word.
The holy melody made the aisles to ring ;
His kingly wisdom shone in every place ;
Maidens to him did rich offerings bring,
And every act he perform'd with love and grace.
The sacred anthem was sung in praise to God
Who reigneth supreme o'er all the earth ;
He loves to chasten with His holy rod
Those who reject the sacred test's true worth.
Now Solomon's song we'll sing with glee,
And bear in memory the author's name,
And give thanks to God in eternity
From whom the *inspiration* came.

ACROSTIC.

As on the path of life you tread,
And as time is fleeting on,
Remember life is a brittle thread
On which to lean upon.
Now may yours be joyful to the end,
So that happiness may spring,
And when you to Hymen's altar wend,
Loud may your marriage bells ring !
Zealous and loving may your bride be,
May the pleasures of life be given,
And when your spirits from hence flee,
Ne'er miss the route to Heaven !

THE GILDED DOME.

Behold yonder dazzling, gilded dome
On stately mansion crown'd ;
It is the proud and rich man's home,
Where pity for others is never found.
But luxury and foul dark vice
Contaminate its terraced walls,
Though 'tis adorned with art so nice,
And magnificent its costly halls.

And hollow hearts therein dwell
Ne'er known to charity given,
Naught but vainly fashion's swell,
With ne'er a glance to Heaven,
The earthy of the earth doth reside,
And run sinful riot there ;
Its portals are not opened wide,
For the poor they have no care.
Folly and pride the gallants sway
In the frescoed rooms of wealth,
There the passions have full play,
Which undermines the victims' health.
Glittering gems of rarest value
Adorn the breast of the foolish rake,
Who with high-born damsels loves to dally,
Dressed in fine lace for fashion's sake.
A pandemonium quite often reigns,
And the household in uproar rises,
For a Xantippe mistress therein gains
Scandal's foul, notorious prizes.
They're not given to hospitality free,
Because from selfishness they'll not depart,
Nor to their God e'er bend the knee,
For *Gold* is most sacred to each heart.
Like whited sepulchres in human form,
They go ghoul-like through the course of life ;

Though they are shielded from poverty's storm
Yet they spend their time in Pride and Strife.
Such is giddy life 'neath the Gilded Dome,
Where minarets flash in sun's bright rays,
For callous hearts live in that unenvied home,
Who ne'er to their just God give praise.
When on death's bed they're hardened to the last,
Though God's mercy is held out to save,
Yet ne'er a look to Heaven they cast,
But sink unlov'd in the sinner's grave.
Anon, there will rise o'er where they're laid
A costly monument of fine artistic art,
Telling the virtues they've done and said ;
But marbled script can't change a once vile living
    heart.

THE COTTER'S HOME.

(A CONTRAST.)

Now let us visit this low-roof'd cottage nigh,
  With vines trellised o'er its humble door,
And tasteful garden in the lot close by ;
  Its tenant is a laborer poor.

Tho' rude the furniture it adorns,
  And all its contents are commonplace,
Yet here are *heart roses* with no *thorns*
  To prick to the quick, or flush the face.

Contentment reigns, and hush'd repose
  Tranquillizes the good inmates here ;
Pure affection soothes all worldly woes,
  Should any by mere chance appear.

'Tis rural bliss free from deep care,
  Each one vies true happiness to impart ;
Their joys they share alike, and each ill bear,
  Divine attributes of the human heart.

No pomp or useless luxury is theirs,
  To mar the blessings of ruddy health ;
No violent passion e'er them ensnares,
  Nor do they lust for Mammon's wealth.

A crust they can spare for famish'd men
  Who by misfortune stroll their way,
And at the offering, now and then
  On the pass'd plate a mite can lay.

No precious gems are set on their breasts ;
  No Ostrich plumes are reared on high ;
But the May-day beauty on her virtue rests,
  To gain the lov'd swain that's standing nigh,

By no manœuvres false do they entice
  Some unsuspecting youth, by vain deceit,
But in open church they're asked thrice,
  So all impediments they can meet.

At morn they rise from refreshing sleep ;
  Laborious is their toil from day to day,
And oft the sire is in reflection deep,
  How to regulate expenses in a frugal way.

No hereditary disease lurks in their blood,
  Nor effect of follies from youthful days
E'er saps their strength, which has withstood
  Wrestling bouts of rude athletic ways.

No rustle of silk is heard down saintly aisle
  When the fair maidens to church e'er go ;
The sting of shame ne'er them doth defile,
  They kneel in reverence, and not for show.

Not in man alone they put their trust,
  But on their Creator they e'er rely ;
They let the sword of unrighteousness rust ;
  In virtue they live and in peace they die.

LINES ADDRESSED TO CAPT. W. W. KIDDLE.

(LATE OF THE WHITE STAR LINE STEAMER "CELTIC.")

FRIEND, we parted off Ceylon's fragrant Isle,
  Each a different course to steer,
In friendship's grasp and sadden'd smile,
  When the South Monsoon was near.

Our boyhood's home now lays a wreck
  In Orange Bay quite deep,
And Johnson,—Codner, who trod her deck
  Have gone to eternal sleep.

Where are those daring seamen gone
  Who were with us on the sea ?
Some dropp'd off, alas ! one by one,
  Where you and I soon will be.

Time cannot efface memory dear,
  Though us seas and mountains part,
And ofttimes in a passing year
  I've called you to mind and heart.

Our earthly trials will soon be o'er,
  Our departure from hence we'll take ;
Now let us steer for Jordan's shore,
  For our dear Saviour's sake.

SEA SONG.

Boreas, give us a flowing sheet,
  With strong breezes abaft the beam,
And we'll belay on the oaken cleat
  Though waves dash o'er a stream.

The yards are pointed to the wind,
  The topping-lifts hauled tight,
And though our sweethearts are behind,
  We'll drink their healths to night.

We'll sing the old sea-songs, my boys,
  With loud chorus chanting free ;
Old Neptune will listen to our noise,
  For 'tis " Saturday night at sea."

Yes, " Saturday night at sea," hurrah !
  We'll sing to the old sea-god,
And drink to them that are far away
  Upon our dear native sod.

And when the short dog-watch is o'er,
  And eight bells have all been struck,
We'll take a parting drink once more,
  And toast all hands, " Good luck."

CREATION THE WORK OF GOD.

Where'er we stray, O God, we find
Some marks of Thy almighty hand;
The beasts and birds of every kind
Thou hast spread o'er every land;
The rocks that scientists doth unmask,
That have lain hidden long ages past,
From whence didst they come? ourselves we say,
For on each atom Thy stamp is cast.
Thou—First Cause—earth's foundation laid,
Thy wisdom stands in bold relief;
Man in Thine image Thou hast made,
And of all creatures madest Thou him chief.
How majestic is yonder ocean grand,
Whose crested billows rolling bound!
And polished shells on sea-beach sand
Tell where Thy curious works are found.
The whale that spouts and sports in seas
Was formed in strange proportions great;
He stems the currents and the breeze;
Contrast—pilot-fish that on sharks wait.
In the firmament high we see the stars,
And bright planets in their orbits course,
And in the comets, meteoric wars
From them we trace their divine source.

Orbs in geometrical symmetry range,
Through vast space in innumerable ways.
To us Thy works are grand and strange
As we note the sun's bright dazzling rays.
From natural laws we look to Thee
As the true means of this great power,
All sprung forth by Thy high decree,
From sturdy oak to tenderest flower.
But where beginneth and endeth space?
Alas! 'tis not comprehended here,—
Maybe Thy angels in their winged race
Knoweth the confines of universe's sphere.
But to mortals that knowledge is not known;
Even imagination no limit can set,
Yet when Thou bestowest Thy angelic crown,
That knowledge in heaven man will get.
God, our Father, we Thee devoutly hail,
And trace epochs back, as delving sceptics can.
Yet all their subtle logic will not avail,
Unless they prove whence came *first germ* of man.

LINES WRITTEN IN A LADY'S ALBUM.

A loving task of friendship true
I write upon this page,
And I shall ever remember you
From youth to olden age.
Your kindness I shall ever prize,
Your lovely manners esteem,
May your reward be from the skies
Where Heavenly glances beam.
May God grant a ray of Holy love
Your future life to bless,
Shall be my prayer to Him above
And for best of happiness.
In future years, when olden age,
Hath crept on in Time's swift flight
Should you by chance turn to this page,
Keep me in *Memory's* sight;
For I shall ever think of you
In Peace or War the same,
So let this be a token true,
For herein I write my name.

DULCI ET DECORUM EST PRO PATRIA MORI.

Elegy on the death of Elias M. Mercer of Co. "F," 2nd Regt. of Oregon Mounted Volunteers, who was fatally wounded at the battle of the "Meadows," April 27th, 1856.

'Midst din of battle on the mountain steep,
 The dusky foe with unerring aim,
Who through the brush did silently creep,
 Sent the *Volunteer* to endless fame.

When mortally shot at duty's post,
 They bore him o'er the craggy steep,
A sturdy phalanx—that warlike host,
 And to guard him safely discarded sleep.

Then toiled thro' forest's snow-drifted path,
 And crossed swift streams in their angry flood,
While the elements vented forth their wrath,
 Yet they surrounding foes withstood.

Alas! Virginia's son died on Umpqua's soil,
 And now sleeps calmly 'neath the sod,
Honorably freed from a soldier's toil,
 Made an angel sentry by his God.

He fell where heroes are *only* found,
 At the front of battle he gave his life,
And o'er him *we've* raised on yond' green mound,
 A memento of how he fell in the strife.

UNSEEN POWER.

(AN APOSTROPHE.)

ERUPTIONS that have changed old Neptune's wide do-
    main,
Would a fiery tale unfold of Islands newly made,
Tall peaks have rose from the deep, to tumble o'er
    again,
And submerged forests in the North Sea are deeply laid.
Mountains fall by avalanches suddenly sweeping down ;
The Alpine steep for ages changing nature's rugged face,
And making the scenery wear yet more an awful frown,
Whose rudely heights mountaineers oft love to chase.
By nature's aid the sun's expansive rays split the granite
    rock
From out the mountain side, when contracted by cooler
    air ;
The sudden influence hurls the mass down with roar-
    ing shock ;
By nature's laws it fell, but nature, tho' changed in
    form, is there.
Silently she worketh, never sleeping, never weary day
    or night.
The crumbling atoms she forms again to suit her varied
    mood ;
Men probe and peer into her realms with visionary sight ;

As yet by them her curious ways are slightly understood.

Behold yond' peak which soars towards the sky on
mountain range,

That stands majestic, yet forces are working that it will
change ;

At some future period it will crumble piece-meal and
fall,

Or by sudden convulsion will reach by gravitation the
goal

Which nature, for a time, deems fit to place the towering giant

That had stood for ages amidst the smaller mounts, as
though defiant.

There the broken up remains may lay for an indefinite
age,

Until nature stirs from her calmly mood, and in her
seeming rage

Forces the debris of the once king-like peer of mountain
chain.

From its bed of rest, and make of the fragments an
open plain.

Perchance her freaks instead may be formation of an
ocean's bed,

Or by slow mutations form chains of lakes, each one
by streamlet fed.

Innumerable and mysterious are these upheavals done,
And there are silent workers—electricity and the piercing
    sun.
Visible and invisible are nature's aids as Time is on-
    ward winging,
And as centuries roll round, she, by mighty power, huge
    rocks are flinging.
From whence sprang these forces which modern
    scientists discover,
And matter from inertia of rest, ever changes when
    nature is the mover?
When shall we know the source of power that was
    brought to bear,
And hurl the mountains' weighty mass, or hard rocks
    asunder tear?
What causes these disturbances taken place from time
    without an end?
And how do religionists and scientists their theories de-
    fend?
At this epoch we regret that limited means are at hand
To *show* the " Power behind the throne," that disturbs
    this land.
Chemical action is going on almost unperceived, but
    slow,
And when the mighty thunderbolt is ready nature strikes
    the blow.

Grand cities made by men's architectural hand and
    mind,
From dark oblivious abysses we exhume and duly find ;
Some cindered o'er by showers from Mount Vesuvius
    hurl'd,
A memorable event that astounds the Latin world.
Volcanic action death's tocsin sounded with sudden
    alarms,
When mothers were engulf'd with their offspring in
    their arms,
And that was fiery nature that buried every soul ;
No land is ever sure but o'er it some dreadful storm
    may roll.
We cannot say 'twas vengeance of a merciful just God
Who was chastening His people with chastising rod,
For no time was for repentance granted and none left
    to repent.
Let us hope for His great mercies' sake their souls to
    Heaven went :
And 'twas nature in her most angry mood of fiery rage,
That wrote the ever memorable Herculaneum page.

ODE ON CONTENTMENT.

"There is a time to laugh, and a time to cry,
There is a time for everything to be done;
There is a time to live and a time to die,
There is a time for Heaven to be won."
They that seek Dame Fortune oft find her in the
　　　shade ;
'Tis best to take in season everything on earth below,
For God who has every destiny made,
Knoweth the spring from whence our joys should
　　　flow.
But man is ever eager and anxious to possess,
Craving the dim unknown by covetous desires ;
Perhaps 'tis better that he should have the less
Than his breast be heated by consuming fires.
Contentment is a banquet at which sages feast ;
Frugal habits great wisdom to them impart ;
Alas ! by vain desires men's joys are made the least ;
Luxury oft bringeth sorrow, but contentment balms
　　　the hearts.
Let us improve the time while youth's buoyant spirits
　　　flow,
With sweet peace and plenty smiling all around ;
Let all mankind the seeds of concord deeply sow,
Where the weeds of discontent are often found ;

So that pure happiness undisturbed may bloom,
Radiant with rays of love without dull vain regret,
And all vicious desires to meet sepulchral doom
Before it is too late, and our evening sun be set.
When we lay down to pay the debt which nature
      claims,
May no remorseful phantoms hover round our heads,
To feel we have not played with *Mammon's* enticing
      games,
But to see in vision the angels beck'ning.o'er our beds.
God grant our souls to pass where discontent is un-
      known,   -
Our loved affinities affectionately to greet,
The place where contented spirits have ever flown,
Who worship at their Heavenly Father's feet.

IDYLLIC ODE.

Know ye the land of the myrtle and maple,
That stands in fair groves of nature's rich soil?
They've throve there for ages so firmly and staple,
And circling round their hearts are each yearly coil.
Know ye the land where the wild vines are growing,
Drawing rich sustenance from roots deeply bedded?
Know ye the spot where the mistletoe is showing

Its clinging love for the oak, so closely 'tis wedded?
Know ye the land where the elk loves to roam,
And ferocious bruin in the thicket doth hide,
Near the swift river whose torrents wildly foam,
And the copse where the doe lies with fawn by her
    side?
Know ye the mad stream where the spring salmons
    leap
O'er breastworks of foam in the rapids so high,
Swimming with lightning speed up cataracts steep?
A few reached the goal, but alas! only to die.
Know ye the land where the forest is towering,
The trees' tall spires pointing to zenith's high space,
Where tangled wild-wood is umbrageous, embowering,
Pierced by trails of the deer which hunters oft chase?
Know ye the land of the rugged mountains steep,
Where rocky crags and sharp spurs jut out in relief?
There the wild panther howls or doth stealthily creep,
As he prowleth for prey like a sleek midnight thief.
Know ye the rich glades in the merry green wood,
That like enchanting scenes burst out in full view?
Aye! even stern stoics in amazement have stood,
As they gazed on shrubbery crystallized with dew.
Know ye the land where the gay birds are singing
In ecstasy flitting from green twig to slim spray?
Dame Nature the fledglings with feathers are winging,

And soon from the nest will they all fly away.
But will we e'er know the land told of in Bible story,
Where angels are chanting praises night and day?
Ah! that is the *fair* land—(but not for vain glory),
'Tis only for them God hath invited to stay.

CONTEMPLATION.

(AN INDIAN'S SOLILOQUY.)

FROM this craggy mount my eyes survey
Tall piny forests and rolling prairies green,
Where the dashing stream wends its rough way,
Which seems to say the Great Spirit here has been.
I mark the trees, their bark, their boughs and leaves,
And yonder far off rock whose caverns screen
Ferocious bears that all winter grieves;
All this tells me, His spirit here has been.
I note the bushes wet with morning's dew,
Sparkling in sun's rays like silver sheen.
I prize my trusty bow made from stoutest yew.
These tell me where His spirit has been.
As I watch yonder clouds gathering high,
Some rolling in blackness whilst others careen;
When lo! His angry voice in thunder tones rolls by,
In awe-struck wonder I list where He has been.

Anon, the sky is rent in twain aloft,
By forked lightning darts and flashes keen,
My heart which fear'd no foe is stricken soft,
Because my vision His fiery works has seen.
I see the quivering snake with venomous mouth
Quick, darting in the grass, fearing to be seen ;
I look to the East, the West, the North, and South,
At every point His mighty hand has been.
I mark the antler'd deer, as he proudly stands
With agile limbs, so lithe and clean ;
I see the roaming elk in numerous bands ;
All these are proofs where He has been.
From this hardy tree poison'd arrows I make,
To fight treacherous foes, blood-thirsty, mean ;
The well aimed arrows will make them quake,
For merciless death tells where He has been.
I see the bright sun soar in the sky
Whose height above, for rude time I ween,
And when I see the full moon on high,
Our traditions say it hath ever monthly been.
I reason that my ancestors' skill never made
The innumerable things in this vast scene ;
My race, though proud, is the merest shade
Compared to what *Thou* art, or where *Thou'st* been.

ODE.

(JEALOUSY.)

As jealousy is the rage of man, and bringeth him to
    woe,

O let us shun its bitter paths as on our road we go !

Let us remember Jesus was beset by jealous men of old,

Yet he pitied them in His meekness, and took them to
    His fold.

For well He knew resentment would add fuel to the
    flame,

As they reproached Him and called Him a drunkard's
    name.

Envy is like rottenness of the bone, and preys upon the
    mind.

O give us patience, Lord, so that jealousy us will not
    blind !

For when envy and strife abound no goodly work is
    done,

But confusion is rife all day from the rising of the sun.

If my friend is superior to me in manner or in his mind,

Let not, O Lord, the feeling of jealousy wound the heart
    once kind ;

But let sweet emulation with all its kindred feeling

Be o'er my soul spread, and friendly love be sweetly
    stealing.

Grant us **Thy** cure from out Thy book that is graced by
    truth and love,
So that our jealous **minds** be **eased by Thy** influence
    from above,   [stingeth,
For jealousy is worse than the **tooth of the adder** that
Or the folds of the snake that **death slowly bringeth.**
But, Lord, we'll trust Thee forever to banish our **feelings**
    of pain,
And **make jealousy flee so it ne'er** enters our souls again.
For jealousy is the rage of man, and surely shortens
    his life,
Entailing woe and despair with embittering strife.
We trust **Thee, O God, that the awful** feeling may flee,
That calmly and meekly we may **ever pray unto Thee,**
And thank Thee in gratitude, **in sincerity and love**
For manifold **favors** showered down from above;
And serenely **may** we **view** the episode of brief life,
Shunning jealousy **forever, all vain** envy and strife!

THE VILLAGE BAND.

See ! the village band is marching ;
    Hark ! and listen to the tune,
Their quick eyes are eagerly searching
    In the book for " Bonny Doon."

Now they're done, to rest awhile,
　But begin with "Annie Laurie,"
A song that's brought both tear and smile
　In trenches of famous glory.

Once more they change to "Sherman's March,"
　The tune that Northern heroes sung
When they Georgia's State did search,
　And their flag to Southern breezes flung.

After a brief rest—then "Rally round the Flag"
　Is played with patriotic strain ;
That ensign floats o'er plain and crag,
　And who will dare its folds to stain !

They've changed again to "Dixie," now,
　The air that fired the Southern's heart,
The tune that helped discord to sow,
　And made rebellion once to start.

Now quick they turn to "Irish Molly, O,"
　A tune for all Hibernians, sure ;
It is the fairest one I know,
　And holds the key to Cupid's door.

Then comes, "Scots wha hae wi' Wallace bled,"
　And each laddie in this music band
Seems as tho' in fancy he does tread
　Caledonia's bleak and heathery land.

Then in unison they play "Britannia,"
  In compliment to Albion's Isle,
Whose many sons have strayed away
  To make the wilderness to smile.

They intersperse with foreign airs
  In semibreves and quavers;
This music soothes the citizen's cares
  And from crotchets they get favors.

Clefs—baritones and tenors bring
  Their sounding notes divine;
Solos on the air vibrating ring,
  And songs they tune of "Sisters Nine."

DE MORTUIS NIL NISI BONUM.

Lines written on the death of the late Captain Wm. Tichenor, Indian
War Veteran, N. P. Coast, Died July 27th, A. D. 1887.

Son of old Neptune, thou hast gone
To the *locker* of the darksome grave,
And friends are weeping all forlorn
At the loss of one so truly brave.
We knew thee in years long sped,
When full of energy and hope;

By death thy cherish'd plans have fled
For which thy mind hadst full scope.
In danger's hour thou wert in the van,
When the Indian massacres were rife ;
Thou shone forth a hero, and died'st a man,
Only yielding to God who gave thee life.
Thou lived not in vain, for yon sea-laved site
Which in early manhood thou boldly founded,
For it thou put forth thy main and might,
And so thy deeds shall be duly sounded.
For 'tis such men as thee, when living,
By acts of daring combined with skill,
Are ever to posterity giving
Tokens of their indomitable will.
But now thou'rt gone, yet thy name shalt live
As one who didst thy country serve ;
Faults if thou hadst man will forgive,
In admiration of thy mind and nerve.
So rest in the tomb where lov'd ones laid thee,
To sleep near the sound of ocean's roar ;
Thy spirit hast gone, by God's decree,
To dwell in peace forevermore.
And may these lines serve as a token
Of the "Muse's" saddened spell,
As if from the lips thou heard'st them spoken,
As we bid to thee our last farewell.

THE PRECEPTS OF THE HOLY LAW.

Come, and I'll tell thee what Maimonides did say,
The philosopher of old to whom minstrels did play,
For he taught our fathers, and expounded God's word,
And told them how Moses was inspired by the Lord.
The Holy Law to Moses on the mountain was given
By Jehovah, whose realm was o'er earth and Heaven.
The texts of the written law in the Pentateuch were wrote,
And the oral law has to each generation been taught.
Moses interpreted it to Aaron in his tent on the ground.
Eleazar and Ithamar also heard the words sound ;
The Elders came, and the text to them was given,
And the people heard the Lord's commands from
        Heaven.
They memorized the interpretation of the word,
And rose in exultation and praise to the Lord.
Oh, let the precepts be imbued on thy heart forever !
And bless the Lord above, the Great Eternal Giver.

ACROSTIC.

So be your lives, that God may bless
To the end of your brief mortal time,
Each other to love and fondly caress,
Protected by Him in this western clime.
Happy may you be link'd in Hymen's chain,
Each round of pleasure to bring you bliss,
No cares to wring your hearts with pain,
And the road of adversity may you miss.
No sickness e'er come to check your joy
Down the hill of life as on you go !
Every phase of life without some alloy
Mankind can not expect to know.
(May God calm for you life's bitter blast
And fit you both for Heaven at last !)
Contented be your lot through life,
Heaven to be the designed goal to win,
And by steering clear of wrangling strife,
Doorways of God's kingdom ye can enter in.
When age creeps on, and death draws near,
In peace may you both lay down to die,
Conscious of your lives unblemish'd career,
Knowing and trusting your Father on high.

THE ADVANTAGES OF A COUNTRY LIFE.

UNDER the veranda, near by umbrageous trees,
An aged father sat with a fair boy on his knees,
The prospect was fair to view, the waving corn afield,
Near by the kine are standing the lacteal fluid to yield;
The landscape is slightly crimson'd by the setting sun,
The rustic swains in glee, their daily tasks are done.
" My son," the father said in deep affection's tones,
"Ere I go hence to rest these weary, tottering bones,
Some good advice I desire to offer unto thee,
So that when I'm dead thou'lt e'er remember me.
This bequeath'd mansion and these fair glades around,
With nature's teeming wealth luxuriantly abound.
Keep thee close to them ; crave not for city life,
And guide thy now pure soul from all vain strife ;
For here thou wilt find comfort with no perplexing
    aim,
Moreover, thou canst hand to posterity our goodly
    name.
A city life for one who has been home and country
    bred,
Oft leads to time and place where thou canst not rest
    thy head,
Nor a haven find whenever circumstances change,
But on this fair domain all thy pure joys can range.

No foul smoky incense here, no false ambition sways,
All here is peace and plenty by God's providing ways.
No visionary schemes to haunt thy mind serene,
But rural contentment is shed on this fair scene.
Here thou canst shun the vicious who on thee would
    prey,
Thou canst keep company with virtuous maids each
    day.
And when the Sabbath comes, to meeting thou canst
    hie,
There learn how thou shouldst live, or be resign'd to
    die
With the hope of immortality which is offered free to all,
And listen fervently in faith to the evangelistic call.
So pine not for what may appear to be so very grand,
O rest and stay on this, thy broad ancestral land,
Where thou canst grow up to man's most noble state ;
Spurn not these good reasons ere it be too late.
Temptation prompts the guileless, and the unwary fall,
List' not to the charmers, though they enticing call.
They sow not neither do they toil, nor spin,
Thou wilt reap tares if thou ever enter in ;
Here thou canst find a partner for thy future life,
A virtuous woman to be thy true-hearted wife.
Ye can remain beneath this sheltering roof
With naught to mar, and none to utter reproof,

But in idyllic gladness the journey of life canst go,
Alike to share your joys or commiserate each woe.
And when your course of life is narrowed down to die,
In the same grave, side by side, we all can lie,
There to await the resurrection of the day to come,
When our spirits will meet in a heavenly home.
But shouldst thou in city's speculations e'er subscribe,
And in disappointment meet with companion's jeer or
    gibe,
Despair may come with passions uncontrolled,
To the wine cup flee, soon thou'rt in the gutter roll'd,
Become an outcast to the world, to sense and duty blind,
And virtuous precepts are left far, far behind.
Or if, perchance, the blind goddess favors thee awhile,
I say, beware of her false, fickle and treach'rous smile.
She clasps her votaries with an outward grace;
The victims yield, but ruin stares them in the face.
This is my last admonition given to thee for good,
For thou art my beloved son in whom courses my own
    blood;
And if thou takest heed, I am content to die,
And in yond' churchyard where thy dear mother doth
    lie,
I'm willing and resigned this mortal frame be laid,
Where the weeping willow casts its sombre, dreary
    shade.

THE LIBERTINE.

WITH polished manners and studied mien,
He stalks around the worldly scene,
His outward grace attractive to the view,
His vices many, but his virtues few.
He looks around to see whom he can devour,
Voluptuously lingers in the lady's bower;
His conscience seared with red-hot iron,
He loves the company of each guilty siren.
The movement of his eyes his covetous will obeys,
He knows womankind's weak and trusting ways;
He'll ingratiate his manners and his mind,
(That he thinks is unequal in this world to find).
He may be rich in gold; that don't atone his vice;
Good society he enters, it is so very nice,
By its association that very act will screen
All his pecadilloes that are likely to be seen.
He's proud, an upstart from his very birth,
Which pride is oft mistaken for meritorious worth.
He will delude his friends when best to be sincere,
The charges that are laid to him can't all be told here;
But then his position in the social scale—
As a refuge there he flees—that ends the tale.
And oft he falls in love, but his love is not sincere,
And that kind of love a virtuous girl should fear;

For he's a libertine, and, sordid, cares for naught
Except to take from innocence that for which crusaders
        fought.
He chuckles o'er the conquests he has made,
But all his conquests have an eye to trade;
Yet perhaps he'll beguile some innocent creature
With every form of virtue in character and feature.
They marry; but what then? we ask;
A time they live in dalliance, and then begins the task;
His licentious habits cannot be shook off soon,
At her appeals for constancy she may talk to the moon.
It was born in him to range the dens at will,
He has the gold, and that can scandal kill.
His satellites around have quite an open palm;
Of course to them it does more good than harm.
But his poor wife at home, left to dark despair,
A prey to grief, and nearly killed with care;
Well, what of her? she's nothing now to him,
And at her entreaties his heart is callous and dim.
He loves to carouse, neglectful of his trust,
While she's anxiously waiting with heart ready to burst.
Now she sees too late, and ekes out her bitter life;
This is the sad end of the libertine's fond wife.
She clasped her babe to her broken-hearted breast,
Unloved she lived, alone she died, now she is at rest;
Now she's dead, to the cold damp grave she's taken,

And the lonely child she left, alas ! is forsaken.
So the libertine goes back to his *idols* so vicious,
For him 'tis daily life, to him it is delicious.
At last he falls sick, disease will cankering kill;
No use of nostrums, for it is the Almighty's will.
Remorse comes on, but contrition can't call back
The one who so fondly loved ; he's tortured to the rack.
A lingering painful death, slow and sure it works,
To him in delirium her spirit hovering lurks,
And gazes reproachfully in his deceitful eye—
Hark ! she calls him traitor to the holy marriage tie !
At last, inquiringly he calls for his friend of old,
That friend steps forth to gaze on the *man of gold*.
In his last throes the hypocrite for mercy cried,
His friend points upward—says "in heaven 'tis denied."
He dies, and laid next to her he had rudely spurned,
Even the worms away from his vile carcass turned.
Perhaps scientists in ages to come this soil will turn,
When he's rotted 'neath the pompous marble urn,
And find the bones of him who died in such distress,
Pronounce them an extinct *Mammon* of an ancient
    wilderness.

MEMORIAL ODE.

Ode written to commemorate the memory of the heroic dead, on the
occasion of decorating their graves with flowers on Decoration
day, May 30th, 1888, at Roseburg, Or.

HERE lie the patriots who bared their breasts to foes
When youth and energy were theirs to spend,
They were comrades of war's terrible woes,
That for freedom's cause willing arms did lend.
And round us are survivors of that awful shock,
That nearly rent our fair land in twain,
But by their valor, when at the front they'd flock,
They did the country's honor maintain.
Yes! the country's honor and its prestige saved,
From dark oblivion's deepest abyss,
For if divided that act would have paved
The way to harrowing echo of despots' hiss.
Alas! in these thin ranks there is many a gap
Which once was filled with loyal life.
Ah! methinks the blood-stained war did sap
The comrades brave that fell in the strife.
They fell as brave men should ever fall,
In defense of right and to punish wrong,
They charged pell-mell at the bugle's call,
And now we sing their funereal song

And one by one as leaves fall to earth,
Your comrades drop their musket hand to die,
We honor them now for their sterling worth,
And to their memory heave a sad sigh.
We now turn to the bodies slowly crumbling here,
Perhaps far, far away from their native sod.
As we strew flowers o'er them we'll drop a tear,
Trusting their spirits are with their God.
No sister's gentle hand passed o'er their pallid cheek,
No mother's kind caress was theirs to feel,
No sympathizing brother cheering words did speak,
When battlefields' sad death our comrades' fate did seal.
No sarcophagus or costly urns are o'er
The bodies of the humble soldiers here.
But we honor them for the toils they bore,
As though Egyptian columns were o'er each bier.
The soldier in the ranks as much risk ran
As plumed warrior on his charger proud.
Though subordinate he proved himself a man,
And his grateful country praises him aloud.
Now we'll strew flowers o'er their lowly graves,
And decorate them as brothers of our own,
And as near them the weird yard grass waves,
We deem we've a token of friendship shown.
So rest in peace, dear comrades in arms,
Till the bugle calls with a heavenly note;

The nation is now free from all alarms,
Because for legal prestige you bravely fought.
Now, kind friends, we'll leave them calmly sleeping
Until another cycle of time rolls duly round,
And we'll leave the drooping willow weeping,
Till we come again to strew flowers on the ground.

TO INDIAN WAR VETERANS.

Address of a superior officer of the Indian department at Washington
to an Indian War Veteran of Oregon, A. D. 1888.

ART thou the Oregon robber whose deeds have reached
    my ears?
When thou waged relentless war as I've understood,
And filled the Eastern mind with horrible fears
When thou didst steep thy hand in innocents' blood.
Like a hound thou track'd the aborigines to their lair,
When morning's light in the East had scarcely beam'd,
And in cold blood, horrid acts did do and dare,
At which thy sleeping victims, never dream'd.
Art thou the monster in human form, of olden time!
Who laughing held the bleeding victim's scalp aloft,
Just stripped from the dusky maiden in her prime,
Whilst thy ruffianly companions stood round and
    scoff'd.

Dost thou not know we ken all thy gory deeds,
Were done in coldest blood, in Occidental land!
Dost thou not know thy exalted country bleeds
For the atrocities of yonder blood-stain'd band!
Yes! the shrieks of the victims reverberated o'er the
      vale,
And it seemed as tho' shuddering angels told us thy
      crime;
Now on our consciences we blushingly tell the tale,
And think thy heart is made of clammy, soulless slime.

THE VETERAN'S REPLY,—STOICALLY.

I AM no robber, and disdain exploits to boast!
Nor have I waged useless war as ye understand.
So free your unsophisticated mind from a demon
      ghost,
For my hands are clear from innocent blood in yonder
      land;
I am no dog that I should track the fleeing prey,
When gray morning's light usher'd in the misty morn
I've done no cold-blooded act by night or day,
No sleeping creatures have I from slumber torn.
I deny that I'm a monster, but human as ye see,
And in my youth would scorn a scalp to take,
But in duty defended woman on mount and lea,
When miscreants would their manhood forsake.

I know not what you think, but you're to reason blind,
For the Occident we held against the hostile foe,
When my exalted country in its duty lagged behind,
And refused us succor in our direful woe.
The shrieks of those victims sounding o'er the vale,
Were from our wives and daughters in deathly tortures
      dying,
And thereby on your consciences hangs a dreadful tale
That in the Annals of History there'll be no denying.
Now, mark ye! The symbol that I wear upon my
      breast
Proves the many perilous days I've yonder spent.
Anon! This spirit will be soothed in immortal rest,
Then all my vengeful foes their spleen may fully vent.

THE DIVINITY OF NATURE.

O Nature, man hath made efforts to define thee by fix'd
      laws,
Framed by his mental power and for future guidance
      made ;
Thou hast been from the beginning God's effective
      cause,
And to thy freaks this world's mutations e'er are laid.

Slow is the march of intellect though often triumphs
    crown,
Rewarding men endowed with acumen keen,
Oft by excavations and shafts in the earth sunk down,
He will discern where anciently thy mighty hand has
    been.
Scientific men disagree when they bend before thy
    shrine,
Theories are put forth different views to disseminate ;
Beyond doubt this world was made by Almighty de-
    sign,
No matter for bygone changes or whate'er may be its
    fate.
We note *material* comes to earth from yond' ethereal
    sky
When hissing meteors with velocity descend with glow-
    ing fire.
If we bar the law of gravity, how do they come to
    this earth nigh ?
Behind mere gravitation there is a *Power* more higher,
Questions in philosophy the minds of fickle men con-
    found,
Though nature's moods are many, there is a spirit in
    man
Which sees as in prophetic dream, and on which his
    hopes are ground,

That he who can make such worlds can also a **Heaven**
    plan.

'Tis not for man to e'er gainsay the works of God above,

For if we gaze on yond' mountain high, or turn unto the
    sea,

Or action of sun's piercing **rays** or e'en yond' flowery
    grove,

All these are undergoing **changes** by God's effective de-
    cree.

Yonder moon, though slowly traveling, makes her in-
    fluence felt

On this mundane sphere, for she repelleth the ocean's
    waves,

As the earth spins swiftly in her natural airy belt.

By her the waters are held back as tho' they were her
    slaves.

Immense pressure is made to bear hard upon the
    rolling sea,

Which checks the waters' flow, by lunar influence 'tis
    done.

Then towards the poles, North and South, the water cur-
    rents flee.

Their greatest points of departure are 'neath the tropic's
    sun.

Antagonism also plays an important part in heavenly
    sky,

'Tis an organism of the universe like motion and life,
Each sun and planet is kept in its orbit place soaring
    high
By constant antagonistic forces of far off stellar strife.
All this we call nature, so curious, wonderful and grand,
That man by these realistic truths is astounded and in
    thought
Will ponder on the source of nature's power on sea and
    land,
Convinced that none but the Great Unknown all these
    wonders wrought.

IN MEMORIAM.

LINES WRITTEN ON THE DEATH OF THE LATE GENERAL

P. H. SHERIDAN, U. S. A.

THE hero of fierce battles rests in a patriot's grave,
His sufferings now are o'er, and all his duties done ;
His warlike spirit will meet those comrades brave
Who drew their sabres, and noble victories won.
Shenandoah's vale henceforth shall know no slave,
For freedom's flag was upheld by Mars' valiant son
Who led the dashing charge midst storm of shell and
    gun.

His name is lauded o'er every land and wave,
And to bring us peace hard contests resolutely fought;
His presence in the perilous charges oft did save
The band of iron men when foes deep strategy wrought.
His worthy deeds on fields of carnage surely did pave
The road to fair renown his martial daring sought,
And dearly was each battle won, by blood and treasure
     bought.

The flag he defended floats half-mast to the breeze,
And the drooping eyes of comrades tell the stricken tale;
Sad is the news that o'er the continent flees :
"Sheridan is no more," words which e'en his olden foes
     bewail.
The symbol of respect is hoisted afar o'er the seas,
In memory of him who in battle was impervious as iron
     mail,   [fail.
Whose motto was to conquer, and whose heart did never

We mourn his death, and the nation bows with grief,
And offers sympathy to friends here he lov'd so well,
The army drapes the colors for its lamented chief,
And solemnly toll the notes of the warrior's funeral bell.
In God's camp on high he'll meet the guard of relief,
Who'll salute the new born angel whilst heavenly anthems
     swell,   [*well.*"
Knowing he did his duty here, and countersign, "*All's*

THE LILIES OF THE FIELD.

" LET us consider the lilies of the field,
How they do grow yet neither toil nor spin."
Spontaneously to nature's laws they yield,
As invisible food from the soil they win ;
Blooming and running their life's swift race,
From tiny seeds they sprung to maturity's stage,
Emblems of purity and elegant grace,
Admired by lovely nymph and learned sage.
Ye toil not, for ye have no cares to dread,
Ye spin not for to hide your snowy charms ;
To all vain impulses of mankind you're dead,
And you gaily thrive in spring's gentle storms,
Unconscious also of your exquisite existence
Though your vitality keepeth strong awhile.
Alas ! like man, your life quickly flees from hence,
Tho' unlike him in this for *you* are free from guile.
How mysterious even sages pause to think,
Wondering what is the *principle* of your life,
At their own miscomprehension abash'd they shrink,
Feeling they are creating a tiresome mental strife.
Florists oft' ponder when ye wilt and die.
(And all your pristine beauty has pass'd away)
Where that life went to which bloom'd so gay in May

Your destiny is to grow apace and bloom,
In strict silence your varied changes pass,
But like most worldly matter your natural doom
Is to become a disorganized human mass.
Ye vanish not entirely, for your dregs remain,
And in other forms chemically converted range,
For *matter* is indestructible, and tho' it briefly wane
In nature's laboratory, 'tis ever subject to a change.

ODE.

THE PIONEERS OF THE N. W. COAST.

AFAR in yonder land Oriental of our clime
Some members of a race of pioneers passed the time,
Discussing pros and cons of an immigrating scheme,
And forth they boldly went to fulfill their daring dream.
They started self-reliant new domains to explore,
Bidding adieu to friends perchance they'd ne'er see more,
Indomitable will and prudence marks their career,
Dangers confront them and enemies are in the rear,
Ambuscades they pass where treacherous foes do lurk;
Even then they do and dare, right onward do they work,
For their motto is "Advance," the wilderness to roam,
To lay the germ of empire to spring from log cabin's
      home.

At last they reach the Eldorado of their hearts' desires,
And discuss the future prospect before their camp fires.
Eureka ! they exclaim as they view the fertile plain,
Intuitively in thoughts their vision sees the smiling grain,
New hopes bring comfort now their toilsome march is
    done,
And the goal of earthly happiness by them seems almost
    won.
With energy and alacrity the primitive cabin is made,
And inside their humble home their worldly goods are
    laid.
Among these goods there is a gift God did give unto man,
It is the Sacred Book that reveals redemption's plan.
Into the weird-like wilderness made dark by savage sin,
The pioneers of progress took the Family Bible in,
That consolation they might find in their new phase of
    life,
And nerve them on to victory in the civilizing strife.
Many anxious days and nights they spent upon the
    virgin sod,
No protection here on earth but their rifles and their
    God.
But here we can't the sickening and bloody tales now
    tell,
How in the bloody strife women shriek'd midst demons'
    horrid yell ;

We'll not depict the quiv'ring forms when maidens look'd
    aghast,
As savage fiends in human shape made that sad look
    their last.
All that is past, and gentle peace now supremely reigns,
And where our race's blood was spilt, now grow the
    shining grains,
They were surrounded by savage foes for many an
    anxious year.
When after lapse of time the race of red men disappear,
'Tis then the fruits of pioneers' toil for posterity doth loom.
Towns and cities spring right up with a business boom,
Fine school-houses and universities and colleges abound,
And best of human happiness in every heart is found.
Men of fine parts are brought forth in the Halls of State,
Commerce and intelligence combine to make the country
    great.
A tribute of praise is due the pioneers for their courage
    and zeal
In giving posterity a heritage to enrich the common weal.
So now we bow in gratitude for the immense debt we
    owe,
For we are reaping rich fruits that the pioneers did sow,
Let us their memory cherish as one by one they die,
Hoping God will reward them all in realms beyond the
    sky.

TO THE RAINBOW.

BEHOLD yond' rainbow with its varied hues,
Whose inimitable colors are gay to view,
  The sun's reflection the hazy sky imbues,
And the arch resplendent all its tints renew.

Evanescent as a ray of light it stays,
As if 'twere a glimpse of Heaven's own scenery there,
  Slowly it dieth out, and dimmed become its rays.
'Tis vanished !   But none can tell us where.

And such is human life, and if moral we would draw,
In this world of strife man rises to his highest state,
  But when his Creator willeth comes the inexorable law,
He fades like the rainbow, and Death is his sure fate.

ADDRESS TO THE DEITY.

O THOU who art beyond this vast space,
All wise Creator of every sphere,
Who twirleth huge worlds in their race,
And setteth man to rule Thy *creatures* here !
We cannot pry into Thy motive so sublime.
That Thou hast mankind here made
To breathe and live and die in so brief a time,
And their works decay and moulder in the shade.

Thy ways are not our ways, O great God above !
And we feel our dependence is on Thee,
But oft Thou hast shown Thy holy love,
Permitting us some of Thy wondrous works to see.
Thou art incomprehensible to us below,
And we only perceive Thee by Thy works of love ;
Thy spiritual features none of us now know,
Nor shall we 'till we reach Thy courts above.
We feel all our actions will be sifted up in heaven,
That we've done in all our lives on earth.
O God, in mercy grant we may be forgiven,
And all be renewed by angelic birth !

ODE TO JERUSALEM.

Jerusalem, once happy land,
  Thy turf grows over thee,
    Now pilgrims from ev'ry strand
  Come devoutly o'er the sea.
    Hail ! Mighty empire of the past,
  Thy children adore thy name !
    Deep in their hearts thy site is cast,
And extoll'd by sterling fame.

Jerusalem, once home of the brave,
Where great patriarchs did roam,
   Pious Pilgrims sing o'er David's grave
Who are far away from home.
   Hail, great Psalmist 'neath the sod!
Your songs forever remain,
   And the tunes are heard by the living God,
When sung in piety's strain.

THE RECORDING OF THE ORAL LAW.

ALAS! when Jerusalem was destroy'd
The people fled from thence far away,
In Alexandria the chosen were annoy'd,
And calamities were rife each day.
But the *learning* of the people was preserved
By their God's almighty hand,
And He in compassion never swerved
And the books were ta'en to Jumnia land.
The *literati* went to Tiberias in Judea,
O'er them presided the "Nasie," of great fame,
He and the Rabbis did Jehovah fear,
And won for themselves an eternal name.

Jehuda, fearing the traditions would be lost,
Wrote the "Mishna," from *opinions* of the learned,
Sparing neither expense nor counted cost,
And for that act great fame from the chosen earned.
Jochanan compiled the Gemara ;
In Tiberias the learned sages did sit
Who on the "Mishna" worked each lawful day,
And "Completion" these wise men named it.
The Babylonians who lived under Persia's King
Scorned the work of Jochanan's tribe,
And from the "Mishna" would neither read nor sing,
And for the work would not subscribe.
At last a council was called of holy men,
Inspired interpreters of ancient writ,
Who rewrote the volumes, counting more than ten,
And the wisdom of the "Talmud" by their genius was
    fit.

SONG.

(ISRAELITISH.)

HAPPY the time when the sons of Israel the *Huggab* did
    play,
And with the *Toph* accompanied their melodious lay,
And mark'd time with the *Sistrum* in concerts so grand
When everything flourish'd in Palestine land.

The S'chalishim with three strings fine notes did sound,
While men and maidens in merry dance went round.
But now where are they gone, those blessed on earth,
Who joined chorus of praise to great men of worth?
They have sunk with their instruments to silent decay,
And we as their offspring sing this solemn-toned lay.
No more kettle-drums shall sound in the battles' array,
For the bold warriors are sleeping that were first in the
    fray.

AN EULOGY.

SMART little "Bertie," so thoughtful and kind,
By the "Muse's" pen shall not be left behind,
  We record her brightness in asking for aid
To paint her loved Church so it shouldn't fade,
  And preserve from decay the house of the Lord
Where ministers expound the true Holy word.
  She went around and made her wants known,
And in charity they aided her wishes to crown ;
  They lent to the Lord but He'll surely repay
Tenfold or more at some future day.
  Now "Bertie" was glad to succeed in her plan,
Light-hearted and happy to her home ran ;

She told to her people the collection was made,
And "Bertie's" good name shall not lay in shade ;
For Jesus hath said in his sweet charity
"To suffer little children to come unto me,"
And let us hope when "Bertie" grows older
That Jesus' love will ever enfold her ;
And may she be a comfort to her kindly friends,
Until to heaven her sweet soul wends.

CONQUIESCAT IN PACE.

Lines written on the death of Wm. Henry Wootten, who died 25th day
of December, 1875, at Victoria, B. C.

Thou restest beneath Vancouver's sod
Near Fuca's sounding sea ;
Thy soul we trust is with thy God.
Now 'tis from thy body free.
When I read in daily "news" of thy death,
My heart was sorely tried,
I read the message with bated breath,
To learn my friend had died.
I knew thee on the "Persia's" deck
When thou wert young and gay,
Our boyhood's home is now a wreck,
Deep sunk in "Orange Bay."

I knew thee on the giddy mast
When mad Storm King whirled by,
And now thy form is deeply cast
Where sea-winds their requiems sigh.
And, one by one, each dear shipmate
The anchor of life lets down,
While the living ones patiently await
God's time for a glorious crown.
When the last trump shall sound
O'er land and Neptune's main,
We pray thou wilt then be found
In God's immortal train.

THE DEPARTED YEAR.

Adieu, old friend, thy time has flown
To realms of the vanish'd past,
And where seeds of happiness were sown,
May they by sadness ne'er be overcast.
But fruitful joys spring up anew
In the years which are to come,
And may our sorrows be so few
'Twill be needless to count their sum.
And may the motives and acts of our lives

To posterity as good examples shine,
Industrious as bees in honey'd hives,
And hewed *square* and *plumb* to marked line.
So farewell, Old Year, thy time has gone
From out the period, but not from mind,
For we'll cherish thine ev'ry day as one
That links us to joys thou left behind.

SONG.

LET us paddle in our light canoe
Upon yonder dashing stream,
And skimming o'er the surges woo
And think of love's fond dream.
We'll run the rapids with delight,
And laugh at dangers near,
And dart into the inlet's bight
Without a sign of fear.
We'll quaff from wood-nymph's babbling cup,
As we o'er the billows skim,
And from the heart, love's nectar sup,
When we to prying eyes are dim.
We'll guide the fragile bark's course,
Through tortuous channels' surge,
By skill with energetic force,
We will our light bark urge.

ACROSTIC—MARRIAGE.

LONG may you live and happy be
On this terrestrial sphere,
United in love,—from all ills free,
Impressed that God is near ;
Secure in His almighty power
And meriting His love,
No friend but wishes you each hour
Divine grace from above.
May you enjoy all earthly bliss
On every land and sea,
Deserving God's ever-kindly kiss,
And the best of wishes from *me*.

THE HOMELESS GIRL.

I WANDER to and fro, and on charity depend
No one to guide my youth or no brother to defend.
Weary at mind, and sick at heart, I trudge from door to
    door,
O God ! it is a pitiful sight to be so very poor !

The rich folks can have joys which to me are e'er denied ;
I've sat at their door-step many times and sadly I have
    cried.

From ladies I've met with kindness as oft their love is
    sure,
Yet it is very hard for me so young to be so very poor.

Sometimes hard visaged folks will give me a stony-
    hearted stare,
For such a one as me they say that they've naught to
    spare.
All their scoffs and insults I have always to endure,
Because, forsooth, they all know I am so very poor.

The school-girls are sometimes good, for kindly do they
    give
A portion of their luncheon so that I might live;
Gentle are their manners, and their hearts feel very sore
To think that one of their own sex should be so very
    poor.

At nights, too, when I've no money to pay for a humble
    bed,
I lay me down to rest with a hard stone 'neath my head.
Before morning's light I rise, for the vans make such a
    roar,
That causes but little sleep for one who is so very poor.

And often I'm awaken'd by rough orders to " move on,"
By a man that is warmly clad, and as fine as any *Don,*

Whilst I am in rags and tatters I'm taken by this boor,
To the nearest City Jail because I am so very poor.

I'm tried before a magistrate, and then to prison sent,
When by this harsh sentence my very brain seems rent;
This mandate of the law sends me reeling to the floor;
Crying, "O my God, have mercy on all the suffering
    poor!"

A PANEGYRIC.

On the late James Montgomery, Esq.,—Poet, Editor, and Patriot.—
    Died April 30th, 1854.

MEMORY brings to mind thy presence before me,
After many toilsome years I've spent;
The oppress'd masses did truly adore thee
When for their freedom thy mind was bent.
In thy sanctum in my youthful days I knew thee,
Ere I was prompted other climes to roam;
Thou hast been in my thoughts on land and sea,
When at "Fargate," in thy *musing* home.
To know thy qualities was surely to admire
Thy kindly heart and intellect so great;
In thy soul was kindled liberty's bright fire,
Which on thee brought the ire of sternly state.
Yet unsubdued thou devotedly fought

The fierce battle 'gainst tyrannic might,
And in the van of action the "Iris" sought
To vindicate man's eternal right.
"Gale," too, thy sterling and gifted friend,
Ye were chivalrously welded in embrace,
The rights of freemen boldly to defend ;
At this epoch the effects of your acts we trace.
To bristling power, ye would never bend,
Thou in a prison's cell fill'd a patriot's place,
And "Gale" to Columbia his way did wend
Hurling back defiance to the tyrant's face.
Alas ! in "Carolina" were heard his last wails,
And for liberty he breathed a fervent sigh,
Montgomery ! The angels, thy spirit now hails,
Where the God thou worship'd sitteth on high.
On "Hallamshire's" mount thou lay down to die,
Where once "Waltheof," the hero bold, did roam,
Who did the warlike Norman often defy,
In defence of his much loved mountain home.
But now thou hast past o'er Jordan's sacred tide,
From thy much prized, secluded home.
With the sisters "Gale," thou art laid side by side,
Yet thou wilt e'er be remember'd by thy "Switzerland's"
    bright tome.

NOTE.—Mr. J. Gale died at Raleigh, N. Carolina, August 24th,
1841. He was one of the first stenographers of Congressional reports.

ODE.

ON THE ADMISSION OF CALIFORNIA INTO THE UNION OF STATES, 1850.

A PIONEER's muse from Oregon greets ye, Argonauts,
Who founded California's splendid State.
Some came o'er plains and some in boats,
Around the Horn to the Golden Gate.
Memory recalls to mind the hurrahs sounded
As the old "Oregon" steamed up the bay,
Her cannon boomed as to windward she rounded,
Bringing the news : "We're a State," Hurrah !
That night the City in gay revelry burst out,
And every citizen, in the highest glee
And ecstasy at being "admitted," gave forth the rousing
        shout,
"From Territorial fetters we're now forever free !"
October was the time set to celebrate the event,
And grand displays the civic board prepared,
In due course of time all pioneers went ;
Both high and low their hospitality shared.
The procession formed and marched to music's strain,
Gay banners flew and fluttered in the breeze,
Loud cheers were given o'er and o'er again,
At the good news that came from o'er the seas.
And as friends sat around the festive board,

Some singing songs of "Auld lang syne;"
Some for their blessings thanked the Lord,
And others drank good healths in wine.
Hark! what is that? the shock their pleasures mars;
Convulsive shook the earth around the City gay
Like unto the thunders of a dreadful war;
"The steamer 'Sagamore' has blown up!" say they.
Alas, too true! 'longside of "Long" wharf she lay,
With human freight on board to Stockton bound,
By scores they met their death, nor time to pray,
And many scalded and mangled too were found.
From pleasure to pain the crowd great anguish felt,
But aid was rendered ere the boat did sink.
At sight of mutilated corpses in grief they melt,
And some were the brotherhood of the mystic link;
As in the grave *we* dropt them one by one,
We shed to their memory "The stranger's tear,"
Hoping their spirits to Heaven have gone
Was the silent prayer of each Pioneer.

TO ROSEBURGH, OREGON.

ROSEBURGH, so beautifully situated and gay,
The "Muse," to thee indites a humble "Umpqua" lay;
Thou nestles 'neath forest hills fringed with green,
Most perfect picture of some fairy scene.

Thou art like an orb that is shining bright,
Casting its dazzling beams to cheer the night.
And the centre of action dispensing good deeds
By legal enactments as the good country needs.
On Umpqua's banks thou stands where our lots are
 cast,
And may thy future fate be as fortunate as the past !
Hoping thy prospective development surely will be
 sought,
And by Capital and Labor peacefully be wrought ;
And remuneration made to them who will unfold
The advantageous position thy lovely site doth hold.
Thou hast been the first home of bright men of the State,
Many jurists, statesmen, and some of talents great,
Whose names in thy archives handed down will be
As a legacy to generations to all eternity.
Thy salubrious climate would Italy almost match,
And in the fishing season anglers huge salmon catch.
Thy founder, too, is hale and hearty like a *rose* full
 blown,
Who has *deeds* of charity often broadcast sown.
Flow on, old "Umpqua," past our city's serene shore,
Each wave that forms on thee we'll ne'er see more.
And as thy flood rushes to the expansive sea,
We be reminded the current of our lives rolls swift like
 thee

And the springs of Helicon in time will become quite
    dry,
So to thee, good city, the "Muse" now says—"good-
    bye."

————————

IN MEMORIAM.

Lines written on the death of S. S. Mann, Esq., late of Coos Co.,
Oregon.   Died in San Francisco, April 13th, 1888.

WE bow in grief, as though we were nigh
To him whose spirit hath gone on high.
   Though distant far his body is laid,
Yet *here* the record of his life was made.
   He served his country ; aye, and served it well!
Which friendly tongues in *Coos* can tell.
   His goodness was done with bountiful eyes,
To ease sad grief and stop orphans' sighs.
   New England's son hath gone to God above,
The heart hath ceased to beat once full of human love.
   A Pioneer now rests on California's shore,
Alas ! whose spirit on earth we'll see no more !
   Adieu ! To thee whom the *muse* admired,
Who by the " divine afflatus " is inspired,
   Yet fired with truth as all our lays should be,
So that in Heaven we may meet with thee.

LINES

HAIL ! welcome day of event so great
That connects fair Oregon with her sister State !
Thrice welcome, you who come the road to view !
All honor to you for 'tis your worthy due !
And may this crowning act bring all great joy,
Prosperity to spring, and no dull cares annoy.
Cementing friendship with an ironlike clasp,
The riches of each state to fairly mutually grasp ;
And the ladies fair who ride o'er this new route
Shall be greeted by friends with welcome shout.
And may the maiden—spinster—also the goodly wife,
Carry good impressions back to last through life !
And may the towns along the line new impulse feel,
By the last spike being driven of the road of steel !
God grant the managers of this gigantic scheme
To realize all the good of the capitalistic dream.
May the employés and employ'd live in peace,
To help each other their happiness to increase.
And when, in future years, posterity looks back,
Feel that they've reaped blessings from united track ;
And when all are called hence to live above,
Be the partakers of God's heavenly love.

REQUIESCAT IN PACE.

Elegy on the late Captain J. A. Richards, an Indian war veteran of
1855.   Died at Roseburgh, Oregon, Nov. 2nd, 1887.

THE old soldier has laid his shield aside.
Alas! life's spear is broke in twain ;
No more he will the ranks now guide,
For God his noble spirit has ta'en.
No more he will command or lead,
In the van of battle he'll be no more ;
Well he performed his duteous deed,
He's fought and won sweet Heaven's shore.
Revered and honored unto the last,
Surrounded by loved ones in sorrow's gloom,
O'er his placid brow affection cast
Its enchanting spell when near to the tomb.
O death, where is thy sting ?
O grave, where is thy victory ?
E'en ye *strike* and *hold* a regal King,
And leave us only—memory's story.

ACROSTIC.

THY voyage of life hath stormy been,
Hard has thy lot been cast ;
Onward thou strode with undaunted mien,
Regardless of the rudely blast.
Disappointment with cankering care
Each step thou took beset.
Rejoice, and all thy ills now bear,
All may be happy yet.
No sparrow falls unto the ground
Denied aid from on high,
E'en for thy ills a balm may be found,
Rewards come by and by.
So shall God's light shine for those in shade,
On the gospel page our hope is laid,
Nor will He desert what He hath made.

NOTE.—Thorder is brother to Anderson, the Danish poet, and is a friend of the author.

MARTIAL MUSIC.

Lines suggested on hearing the "Siege of Vienna" played by a
military band.

THE mustering to battle,
The roll of the drums,
And muskets' quick rattle
When fierce foeman comes;
Hark! loud cannon now boom,
Dashing charges are made,
And dire is the doom
By this war piece portrayed.
When the notes rise and fall,
By imagination 'tis seen,
The breach made in wall
Where the ladders careen.
Silence! for steps lightly tread
That seem marching to parapet high;
'Tis the forlorn hope who is led
By him that's to do or to die.
They mount the ladders so high,
Up the steps so valiant they soar,
The defenders soon them espy,
Along the walls the cannon do roar.
The breach is gained by the brave,
The musketeers fire all around,

They rush, alas ! to the grave,
As forward the foemen now bound.
List ! the carnage of blood is great,
In the square and in the street,
And continues until late
Whenever the stragglers meet.
Now hark ! for the city is ta'en,
'Midst shrieks of women's wild yell,
Who prefer to be ruthlessly slain
As dearly their honor they sell.
Anon—hark to the groans of the dying,
And the rush of those fleeing away,
The fatherless, motherless, crying,
While the victors weak citizens slay !
The heroic defenders are routed,
Alas ! seeking a refuge in vain ;
Even the voices of the victors are shouted
By the music's *imitating* wild strain.
Now a lull in the carnage takes place,
When the order is given to sack,
In the notes of the music we trace
The rattle of the plunder they pack,
The oaths of the soldiers in madness,
The shrieks of the victims they kill,
Then come tremulous strains of sadness,
That are echoed afar o'er the hill.

By degrees the firing is slacking,
The death-dealing work is near done,
Some slight cutting and hacking,
And hurrahs for victory won.
The change to a dirge is quite solemn,
It means they're burying the dead,
In places, perhaps, find a whole column
Piled up, whose blood has been shed.
The bugles are calling "To camp,"
The besiegers all lie under arms;
Hark ! to the sentries' slow tramp.
'Tis a truth that "music hath charms."

THE RESCUE.

HARK ! list to the uproar, and yond' loud-toned shout ;
The sound draws nearer and nearer to the ear,
'Tis fire ! fire, and the staunch brigade is *en route*,
When the heart of the mother trembled with fear.
" 'Tis our mansion on fire ! O God, pity us all ! "
She cried out in her agony of darkest despair ;
On the name of her child in shrieks she did call
With face pale as marble and dishevel'd hair.
She knelt down to pray with tears in her eyes,
And to God fervently called on His great Mercy-seat,

Saying, "O Father ! Thou art good and also art wise !
Save my child from the flames, I implore, at Thy feet !"
Furious was the fire where the child slept below ;
Smoke filled the room where the anxious mother stay'd ;
No escape up above, and with fire the stairs all aglow,
While the engine the water on the fierce fire played.
The ladders were reared by the firemen so brave,
Who mounted, the inmates to take in their arms,
They beckoned to the mother, and gently did crave
That she'd trust to their strength and banish her alarms.
She rush'd to the window and looked on the crowd,
Wringing her hands with her features wrinkled in woe,
Crying in her excitement and misery aloud,
" My child ! my child ! O save my child ere hence I go ! "
" Your child is safe ! " a stalwart fireman cried,
" For 'twas myself who carried the cherub down."
Then on the devoted fireman the frantic mother relied,
Assured her child was safe, banish'd terror's frown.
'Midst cheers of the crowd the hero lands her safe,
And almost bewilder'd she flew to her child,
When she press'd to her bosom the tiny sleeping waif,
Caressing it in accents of endearment so wild.
She thanked the brave firemen, then looked on high,
Said, " Father above us, 'twas Thee I implored,
And Thou heardest my supplicating cry,
And Father, Thou art worthy to be ever adored ! "

ZEUXIA.

(A PICTURE WITH A MORAL.)

BEFORE his easel Zeuxia took his stand,
To paint a picture with a master hand.
The features of an old woman was his artistic dream,
So we'll describe his true and fancied theme.

Aged, decrepit, wrinkled and stooping,
Her form was lean and shriveled, shoulders drooping,
Haggard, blear-eyed, with sharp protruding chin,
Wizened as tho' gaunt famine had made her thin ;
Ghastly bony cheeks most hideous to behold,
And all her features cast in a cheerless mould.
Her skin was sallow-hued, sunken her slobbery mouth,
With flabby lips as tho' parched with blighting drought ;
Her mouth awry and open, her toothless gums dis-
      play'd ;
The sight of such a picture would Xantippe have dis-
      may'd.
Her arms were long, and unsightly knots there grew,
And saffron colored finger-nails the artist drew ;
Emaciation and ugliness were the lineaments of each
      feature
Of the *picture* on the easel of God's much lov'd
      creature.

'Twas finished ; then this great artist stepped back to
    gaze
On the horrifying creature of his fanciful maze.
He laughed !   He gazed astonished, laugh'd again,
Immoderately laughed loud and long, with might and
    main.
Ah ! suddenly a deep pain he felt, and 'midst joyful
    feelings sigh'd—
By the *quick* emotional *reaction* in great agony he *died*.
His laughter at the ridiculous figure of his creative brain
Brought him to death by the uncontroll'd laughing
    strain.

MORAL.

Now a moral we draw from Zeuxia's drawing of art ;
To the youths it does a solemn warning impart,
That when on a journey should they aged persons meet
With stooping gait and tottering weary feet,
Ne'er to laugh or scorn at their scraggy looking features ;
Formerly they were lovely to view, and beautiful
    creatures.
Like yourselves their full cheeks bloom'd with human
    love,
Their eyes shone with light like twinkling stars above,
And with pulses beating as strong as yours are now,
Their life blood quickened to a healthy hearty glow.

For you may become like the picture the artist drew,
When creeping age will bid your youthful blooms adieu,
And should you scoff and laugh, or mockery fling,
Beware ! you may like Zeuxia receive death's darting
        sting !
His talent formed one who in God's image was made,
And the Scriptures tell us all our beauties sure will fade ;
For dust we are and unto dust we will turn ;
All in the likeness of Almighty God we should ne'er
        spurn.
The youth—the adult—the hoary aged the same—
Returns again to dust from whence all mortals came.—
So respect old age, and with veneration greet
Whenever the deform'd and decrepit you chance to
        meet ;
For many bear infirmities which the outside world ne'er
        ken,
Who submissively bow in secret and say to God—
    " Amen."

EPISODES OF THE MARINER'S LIFE.

WHEN on the stormy seas sailors are in glee,
    And jovial and cheerful are the crew ;
    With spirits light they make dull care to flee,
    And many strange sights come to their view:

When gallant ship with lofty sails
Fill'd out with stiff'ning breeze,
And in the hurricane's circling gales
They watch from the high *cross-trees*.
And when the waves are dashing o'er
Her bulwarks, when sailing free,
They stand away from peaceful shore
All ataunto from weather to lee.
They see lightning flashes in the sky,
They hear thunders loudly roar,
When keeping her to "full and by,"
And oft her sails in twain are tore.
In midnight watch, murky and dark,
When close reefed against the wind
Sometimes they sight a star to mark
And then their true position find.
When the deck has been clean swept
By rough seas rolling o'er,
Their hearts to stern duty sure are kept,
Tho' loud may the tempest roar.
The helmsman at morn's watch so dark,
As surging waves roll alongside,
Notes by the binnacle's flickering light
The compass point the ship to guide.
When squalls strike with awful blast,
And the lofty mast goes by the board,

The wreckage to leeward then is cast,
And fouled is every cord.
If a lull comes, then is rigged a jury-mast,
Aloft 'tis raised, and sails are spread,
All standing rigging is made fast.
And by old "Boreas" she's forced ahead.
Slow is her speed with no light sails
To catch the zephyr winds aloft.
Cautious is the captain in sharp gales,
And the top-sails are reefed quite oft.
When in the " doldrums " near the " line,"
And sails are flapping fore and aft,
The sea like a mirror then doth shine,
And no ripples are seen in *wake* abaft ;
The porpoises play and sport in glee,
'Neath the bows in " schools " they dart,
Harpooners to weather and to lee,
Pierce the " sea-cow " to the heart.
When look-out man at mast-head high
Spies a *stranger* in horizon's gloom,
Loud in stentorian voice he'll cry,
" Sail ho ! " when off lee bow she'd loom.
As she draws near they signalize ;
The answer is hoisted, " In need of stores,
On their kindness she relies.
Quick relief-crew bend to the oars.

Anon, the farewell signal is given
At dog watch she becomes a speck.
The hope of reward is assured in Heaven,
For charity bestowed on the stranger's deck.
They sight poor wretches on the dreary sea,
Who've been from some ship cast away.
Whose frail raft was drifting to the lee
As helpless and sea-washed they lay.
They lay the main top-sail to the mast,
And soon the good ship's way is stay'd,
Quickly rescuing each starved outcast,
Then on her course the ship is laid.
On the raging deep they often see
Humanity's blessings freely poured,
The weak to the strong for succor flee.
And Pity is oft in a rough bosom stored.
When fever-stricken ship at sea is spoke
Whose "medicine stores" have given out,
When dreaded contagion themselves may yoke,
Then for *volunteers* the mate will shout.
Disdaining self, away they speed,
And by a line to *windward* send aboard
The saving drugs they stand in need ;
'Tis such acts that should be with cheers encored.
Sailors when pacing deck in thoughtful strain,
Running down the trades on even keel,

Their hearts will be far away o'er the main
To those for whom they affection feel.
And when " Homeward Bound " with hearts so light,
They feel for their " Native Land " that throb
Of nature—which to all good men is right—
Such feelings tyrants even from a slave can't rob.

AN EPOPEE—LIFE ON THE FRONTIER.

HARK ! to yond sound on the mount's high range !
The yells are terrific, most hideous and strange.
Ah ! 'tis the war-whoop and the foe on the path !
He is seeking revenge in red painted wrath !
And here unprotected, alone, we've to stand
To battle for home and our dear native land,
No help but our fortitude and courage as well,
To meet and defy that inhuman wild yell.
O, great God, to thy care my offspring I leave,
My dear wife and kindred I hope will not grieve,
At my absence to join in volunteers' slim array,
In a sparsely settled country in the hostile affray.
But what we lack in numbers we'll make up in skill,
And by our superior aim many foemen will kill.
'Tis on the defensive henceforth we will act,
And fight for our lives with frontiersmen's great tact.

Now we march to the battle on the trail,—single file,
O'er deep craggy canons in skirmishing style.
The bloody battle is fought, and the victory won,
And away to the forest routed red men swift run.
We bury our dead, and for last solemn rites tarry,
When we march back to our homes with our wounded
       to carry ;
We arrive at our cabins, grim, ragged, and torn,
Cheered by our friends we had left so forlorn.
We gently break the news to the friends of the slain,
And hie to peaceful pursuits 'till they break out again.
After a few anxious months' toiling and scouting around,
Then again on the mountain we hear the war-sound,
When a sad repetition of bloody strife again comes,
Then we haste to the war to defend our lone homes
They call it patriotic, and as leading to fame,
But it is carnage and privation that getteth the name.
O God, what a contrast there is in men's lives !
For some of thy beings seem to be always in gyves,
They're fetter'd with woes which are hard to withstand,
Especially when battling with a blood-thirsty band.
We sigh for sweet peace that to us is a star
More beautiful and pleasing than desolating rude war,
So that industry may be rewarded and affections may
       bloom,
And the red hatchet be buried forever in the tomb.

SONG.

Away to the forest where the wild torrents roar,
Away to tread trails that wild Indians have wore,
Away to the glades where the deer love to roam,
Away to the lodge of the Pioneer's home!

Away to the fairy dell in the deep shade,
Away to meet there my dear loving maid,
Away to the arbor of bold Cupid so sly,
Away to sweet Hymen and stern parents defy!

Away to Elysium's gay shady bower,
Away to happiness without lucre's dower,
Away from scenes of our childhood so dear,
Away to confront the harsh world without fear!

Away to enjoy life with the maiden I love,
Away! for our future lives are shielded above!
Away from the deceit that round us abound,
Away! for true bliss we will then have found!

SONG.

Thoughts of other days spring up
   When youthful joys were ours,
And sweet nectar we did sup
   Beneath the shady bowers;

When youth and joy were ours to share
  With kindly friends around,
No signs of sadness e'er to wear,
  For mirth did well abound.

No folly rent our peace of mind,
  For virtue was our aim ;
Affection round our heart's entwin'd
  And we won an honor'd name.

ON DEATH.

(A SOLILOQUY.)

AND what is death that we should fear his dart ?
If he strikes swiftly our woes will soon be o'er ;
He steers no compass course shaped by mortal's chart,
But strikes his victim on rough seas or tranquil shore.
Why should we sorrow when from friends we part,
Whose life-long virtues we truly did adore?

In time the messenger comes gliding on the trail ;
With stealthy steps he tracks each ebbing life,
And causes human anguish 'midst deathly wail,
Surely he is the victor in the harrowing strife !
And as the gentle spirits of his victims fail,
He cuts the slender thread that holds the span-like life.

All men must die, but God grant it be *one* death
Let it not be one thousand in our lingering span.
Death is an athlete that is never out of breath,
But reaches the goal at last by nature's sternest plan.
His victories are ne'er crowned with laurel wreath,
And true is the aim of the chief of *Hades* clan.

Tis useless pleading 'gainst his inexorable law ;
He is invincible, and when sharp his sickle has struck,
In his mandate we find no sign of flaw ;
Tis his delight in epidemics to run a-muck.
Then he bringeth forth the most calamitous woe,
And vampire-like, life's blood he loves to suck.

LINES ADDRESSED TO WILLIAM WAKE, ESQ.

(OF OSGATHORPE.)

To you, kind friend of olden time,
My muse in deep respect has turned ;
I well remember when in your prime
The esteem of all true men you earned.
No false pride entered your good heart,
And though far from your presence I write,
If a kindness you can impart,
I believe you'd do it day or night.
Our sires were friends of the olden school,

Whose spirits have long since passed away,
They followed the precepts of the golden rule,
And lucre did not their spirits sway.
Adieu, for our time here can but be brief,
And may *your* last days be spent in peace !
Now you're in the sere and yellow leaf
And may God grant you a heavenly lease !

LOW ASH.

WHERE are those joyous spirits now,
That used in thy precinct to stay ?
Their souls were filled with a heavenly glow
Too pure for mortality's clay.
Alas ! methinks some are at rest
Beneath some churchyard's stone ;
Maybe some in this life are blest,
Exalted in high circled zone.
Some of those spirits have roamed no doubt,
In lands of far foreign clime ;
This life has many a varied route
For mortals to spend their time.
Our good, kind tutor has gone away,
His noble wife too,—a lady fair,—
They did our youthful minds once sway,

With most assiduous care.
We that are left remember sure
The garden and round grass-plot,
And the salubrious air so pure,—
" Low Ash," thou'rt not forgot.

BIBLE BLESSINGS.

My Bible I will.read aloud
To them who cannot read,
And chase away the darken'd cloud
That ignorance doth breed.
And as I understand the text
To the poor I will explain,
Although their souls be sorely vex'd,
It will banish heartfelt pain.
Despondency may cause them grief,
And their sins may heavy weigh;
God will bring them sure relief,
And drive their cares away.
Holy Bible, book divine,
Thy sacred page is full
Of loving words in every line,
And blessings there we cull.

SONG.

O WHERE shall my sweet child rest?
For parted soon we'll be ;
May she by truest love be blest,
From sorrow e'er be free !
Where will she go as years onward roll?
Ah me ! I cannot tell ;
Deep-seated grief will fill my soul,
And life be a broken spell.
Where will she be when I am old,
And feeble is my frame?
I love her more than Ophir's gold,
Though changed be her name.
Where will she be when I am dead,
And laid beneath the soil?
She'll think of all the words I've said,
And bear in mind my toil.
I pray thee, God, to bring her rest,
For I truly trust Thy love ;
With Thee I know she will be blest
And shielded from above.
That feeling is consoling now,
To think Thou lovedst my child,
Else, Lord, 'twould be a terrible blow
And send me raving wild.

HAPPINESS.

Behold yond mansion in umbrageous shade :
'Tis fair to view with minarets of gold ;
To its hospitable portals a winding road is laid,
And beds of rare flowers its gay borders hold.
Inside the domain works of art are there,
The hall is strewn with relics of the chase,
The poor from rich tables get a bounteous share,
And leave with grateful heart and smiling face.
The gallery with fine paintings high is hung,
Rich tapestry drapes in decorated rooms so gay,
Where melody is poured forth and operas sung,
And the wassail bowl is drank with wild hurrah.
Within luxurious parlors wealth and beauty vie,
To add splendor to the happiness of home,
And love doth reign with no regretful sigh,
And peace and virtue smile beneath its dome.
The retainers' lives are passed in merry mood ;
No city cares come cankering to their souls ;
In their retirement no *envy* fires their blood,
But high aloft they toss the wassail bowls.

A REVERIE.

How wonderful and acute is the intellect of man !
Throughout long ages his knowledge has augmented.
Though his life is but a brief and fickle span,
He has hard problems solved and deep science entered.
What is *he* that to *him* alone great mental power is
    granted ?
For he's a pigmy in stature to others of God's creatures ;
From the cradle to the grave by curiosity he's haunted ;
Ah ! but he has the image of his Maker in his features.
He's endowed with deep penetration, and meditation
    great,
When guided by logical reason, great are the returns ;
Branches of science and mechanism are brought to a
    perfect state,
And like Alexander for more worlds to conquer his
    heart e'er yearns.

REASON VERSUS BIGOIRY.

Behold yond towering rock that has for ages stood
The onsets of raging storms, of Winter's angry flood,
Inorganic and motionless its various elements show ;
Nature compressed its first atoms by process still and
    slow.

She subtly compounded particles of silicic and sand,
Lo! now it beareth the impress of a Master's mighty
      hand!
/e cannot fathom its massive base, or how deeply it
      doth lie,
As it rises from its primitive bed, in stature soaring
      high.
And with those tiny grains assiduously nature work'd,
Moulding its characteristics like a fairy spirit she lurk'd.
Of her many mysterious ways man but few can ever
      scan,
Although her domain is oft invaded by scientific plan.
To Thee, O God, creator of this spacious whirling
      realm,
We bow in admiration, for Thou holdest the guiding
      helm.
We can turn our thoughts from rocks to jungle's thick-
      set shade,
And note the numberless creatures Thou, O Lord, has
      made.
Toward yond vast firmament in wonder we can look,
And read the stellar sky as 'twere from a heavenly
      book ;
Then in deep contemplation our thoughts can soar to
      Thee,
Who ruleth all these worlds in supreme blest majesty ;

And as we turn away our gaze from scenes grand and
    sublime,
We feel Thou wert infinite from beginning of all time.
Even from rocks and living creatures we can read Thy
    holy name ;
Natural and spiritual laws to trained minds are e'er the
    same,
And this moving sphere revolving on its axis, round
    and round,
Yet we see not its motive power, and we hear not a
    single sound.
Some laws of the universe Thou willest man should
    know,
As yet in Thy wisdom this rare knowledge cometh
    slow.
We thank Thee at this era enthusiastic men can ex-
    plore
The sky, the earth, vast seas, and delve in the fossil'd
    shore,
To examine Thy wondrous works by latest theories
    given,
And by Thy power of exaltation wed the souls of men
    to Heaven.
Now all can pursue and advocate their theories grand
    and fresh,

Without fear of persecution, or being caught in the
    bigot's mesh,
As were Bruno, Copernicus, Galileo, of ancient fame ;
Each one has left to posterity an immortal, noble name.
Some were burned and tortured in that dark and ob-
    scure age ;
But they daringly tore out the leaf of bigotry's be-
    nighted page,
By proved sciences known to man now living on this
    sphere,
We know God's handiwork (unsuperstitiously speaking)
    . has been here.
In love forever He is working man's knowledge to in-
    crease,
And from hidden recesses of nature slowly her secrets
    He'll release.
Perhaps 'tis His will and pleasure when man's spirit can
    it retain,
The real phenomena of the universe He will to him
    explain.
Kingly lips have said that there is nothing new under
    the bright sun,
And saints have taught there is a season for everything
    to be done ;
Lord, grant us true knowledge that will lead our minds
    to Thee !

Also that agnostics and sceptics Thy glorious works
      may see !

And so beholding be convinced Thou rulest Heaven
      and earth,

And for the love Thou hast for man, gave us Jesus of
      virgin birth,

That all mankind should worship and bow to thy holy
      name,

For like unto nature's workings from Thee His great
      powers came.

HINDOO MYTHOLOGY.

BRAHMA was kept inside an egg, but by *power* of *thought*

He broke the egg in halves, that had held him in ages
      past,

Which had confined his spirit and his *mind* his freedom
      brought ;

For three billion four hundred years, in the egg he had
      been fast.

From the two halves of egg he fashioned heaven and
      earth,

Then he created man, who called forth from chaos, ten

"Heavenly Sages," who created bad spirits and spirits
      of worth,

Also, the Sages created the "Gandharven," and Apsa-
      rasen.

Then Brahma, like a pious hermit, from his work did
     retire,
To lead a godly upright life all his remaining days.
" Lotus-eyed " Apsarasen were required by magic and
     lyre,
To try and induce Brahma to change from his godly
     ways.
But the Apsarasen's enchanters had certain bounds not
     to exceed,
So as to cause *any holy man* his solemn vows to break ;
For the anger of the gods would descend without
     mercy, indeed,
And on them severe chastisement sternly would wreak.
But the beautiful Apsarase Rambha succeeded alone,
To turn pious Brahma from his vows of hermitage,
When she was punished by being turned into a stone,
For the incensed gods were all in a terrible rage.
At last the Apsarasen with the Gandharven united,
And conjointly they managed the mad gods to amuse,
To all the feasts of the gods they were cordially invited,
And with merry songs and dances did good humor in-
     fuse.

NOTE.—The Hindoos, believing in the supernatural effects of music,
as well as that the sound was agreeable to the gods, surrounded their
heaven-god, Indra, with hosts of performing genii called "Gandharven," and with female dancers and performers called "Apsarasen."

HYMN.

(EVENING.)

We seek God's counsel from on high
  Where angels dwell in peace ;
To Him we turn with hopeful cry,
  Our burdens to release.

If we would follow His holy creed,
  And our hearts are quite sincere,
Then He'll tend and help in need
  All who His great name fear.

His commands He has handed down
  For His children to obey,
And He on us will cast His frown
  If we ever them gainsay.

Good Lord, we ask Thy aid this night,
  That we observe Thy way,
To keep us ever in Thy sight,
  That we go not far astray.

And as we lay us down to sleep,
  Pray watch us through the gloom,
That when the morning star doth peep
  We wake not to sinners' doom.

HYMN.

(FOR THE SICK.)

LORD, I'm enfeebled on this bed,
  Weak and helpless here I lie ;
All the joys of life have fled,
  O pardon me before I die !

Jesus died that I might live ;
  On His cross I now rely ;
Lord, my spirit Thou receive,
  But pardon me before I die.

Friends around are struck with anguish,
  Some do weep and some do sigh ;
On this bed I toss and languish,
  O pardon me before I die.

Let me feel Thy love is o'er me,
  For Thy word tells the reason why,
That Jesus died by Thy decree,
  That we be pardon'd ere we die.

I leave friends here, but when I'm gone,
  Hear them when to Thee they cry,
So their hopes may rest upon
  A pardon from Thy hand on high.

Now I will try to sleep awhile,
  For to my soul Thou drawest nigh ;
I seem to see Thy angels smile,
  And saying—"Come join us by and by."

HYMN.

(MORNING).

WHEN my eyes awake, lo, I behold
  A glorious scene, O God !
The sun away misty clouds has roll'd,
  And his warmth falls on green sod.

Night vapors vanish at his rays,
  And every thing I see
Fills my soul with wondrous praise,
  And glory unto Thee.

I know how feeble man is here
  In this our earthly vale,
To his wants Thou wilt give ear,
  If he tells his sorrowful tale.

I ask Thee to guard me all this day
  From danger and foul sin,
That when Thou callst me hence away
  Thy kingdom I can win.

I ask Thee to guide my friends aright
    Each day they live below,
That when they enter in Thy sight
    They'll see Thy Heavenly glow.

HYMN.

(MISSIONARY).

CHRISTIANS, arise ! for benighted nations groan.
Go teach the way of salvation in each zone ;
Teach them that our Saviour died for all
Who are repentant, and on Him will call.

Fling out the banner with the holy cross ;
Tell the pagans in deep oblivion their idols toss ;
Exhort them to obey the holy written word,
And the sword of righteousness on their loins to gird.

Go ye, saint-like men, to wilderness's shade,
Go ye to your dusky brethren God has made,
Dig and delve in the mines of deistic sin,
So that God's grace can fully enter in.

Break the stony idols that in their temples stand,
And let the Bible be in every pagan's hand,
And come, sweet sisters, of our exalted race,
Help us to wipe out this dreadful sad disgrace.

The heathens call on mountain and on plain ;
There let us plant Christ's banner ever to remain.
It's stood the test of ages, and *will* till trump shall
    sound,
When our bodies will raise again from the sea and
    ground.

HYMN.

FAIN would I fly to thee, my God,
    For comfort and for rest !
Grant me consolation from Thy word,
    To make me eternally blest.

Surrounded by sin in every form,
    O shield me from its bane,
That I may avert Thy angry storm
    So that I may Heaven gain.

I know I am a sinful worm
    That can be trodden down ;
When first my life began its term
    The seeds of sin were sown.

To Thee I lift my heavy eyes,
    To Thee I appeal in faith,
To Thee I offer up my cries,
    To avert Thy bitter wrath.

Let me the wicked paths e'er shun,
   To turn away from venal guile,
That when my race is duly run,
   Thou'lt grant Thy gracious smile.

HYMN.

THERE are good tidings waiting
   For them who obey the Lord,
And sinful ways are hating,
   And study His good word.

O yes, the Messenger was sent
   To teach the Heavenly road,
Who to the crucifixion went
   To lighten our heavy load.

Then the evangelists afar went
   To preach what Jesus taught,
To help the weary and the faint
   Each one his testimony wrote.

Their proofs have not been shook
   For near two thousand years,
And that holy inspired book
   Has brought infidels to tears.

O yes, the tidings spread around!
Let the Nations hear the news!
Hark! listen to the glorious sound,
Descending like heavenly dews.

HYMN.

Lord, when thou'rt displeased, rebuke me not,
Avert thine angry frown from me;
All my transgressions I pray Thee blot
From out Thy book eternally.

I know I'm weak and prone to sin,
And leave the paths Thy saints have trod;
To Satan's ways I'm more akin,
Than to worship Thee, my living God.

O let Thy anger be kept in place,
Pour it not down on me, Thy son;
For I will my sinful steps retrace,
And repent of all the sins I've done.

Hear me, Lord, with thine ear of grace,
List Thee to my calling voice;
O turn not away Thy holy face!
Let me aspire to become Thy choice.

My sins are heavy, they weigh me down,
  Sad is my soul 'till I call on Thee ;
Let me put on Thy Heavenly crown,
  That Satan from my soul may flee.

I humbly pray on bended knees,
  With clasped hands I make appeal;
Henceforth I'll bow to Thy decrees,
  If thou wilt my transgressions heal.

Make my spirit more tranquil, Lord,
  Soothe passions lurking in my breast;
Expound to my soul Thy holy word,
  And make me number'd with Thy blest.

Now I praise Thee, Jehovah great,
  That knowest the frailties of us here ;
The Messiah didst us reinstate
  When He was pierced by the soldier's spear.

Holy ! holy Lord God above,
  In Thee my faith shall ever be,
For Thou art full of Heavenly love
  And reignest in Eternity.

HYMN.

(TUNE, "THE WATCHER.")

CHRIST gave His life as ransom
   To deliver us from sin ;
And He so Heavenly handsome,
   Man's atonement He did win.

He reconciled our Creator
   By offering His blood ;
And then in three days later
   Before His Father stood.

He sacrificed Himself for all,
   No matter of what degree ;
And when we read the Gospel call,
   We find Pilate's dire decree.

His enemies cried aloud in din
   To crucify God's Son ;
The rabble was deeply steeped in sin,
   Yet He salvation won.

And we'll ne'er forget the bloody knoll
   Where He suffered for mankind,
Good Lord, Thou saved every soul
   That is not to error blind.

We ask God's blessing as we sing
    Good praises here below ;
To Emanuel, Saviour, God and King.
    In humility we bow.

HYMN.

GREAT God of Heaven, supreme Judge of earth,
    We bow at Thy shrine of holy light,
Our souls are struck as with a dreary dearth,
    Take pity on us in our sinful plight.

Tormented by vain hopes and fears,
    Oft torrents of passion consume our souls ;
In grief we live, and with eyes fill'd with tears,
    To Thee we present our suppliant rolls.

Turn not a deaf ear to our earnest cries,
    O give us relief from this weight of sin !
Hear our repentant and harrowing sighs,
    And to our souls let Thy spirit enter in.

We seek Thy face ; let us not sigh in vain ;
    We ask Thy love, though undeserving now ;
Under the influence of dark passion's bane,
    Disobedience has caused us sins to sow.

Lord, let our Redeemer console us here,
  Send Him with Thy halo of light for all;
With Him for our friend we will not fear,
  Nor shall Satan's vengeance us appall.

Again at Thy footstool now we kneel,
  In humility and shame to Thee confess ;
Thou knowest how wretched now we feel,
  O do Thou us forgive and forever bless !

HYMN.

I ope my eyes, and lo, behold,
  I see God's gifts around !
Delightful scenes my eyes unfold,
  For His goodness doth abound.

Tho' born in sin and sorrow's lot,
  Yet His benefits ever shine ;
By God the penitent is ne'er forgot,
  His love doth e'er entwine.

Tho' sown in weakness here below,
  God by His power can raise,
And all His glorious works do show
  He merits our constant praise.

As chaff before the wind we fly
    From the doom of dark despair,
And call on Him that lives on high,
    With sweet angels in His care.

Holy—holy Lord, above the cloud,
    We cry aloud for very shame!
Thou exaltest the humble and lowerest the proud,
    That dare to scoff at Thy name.

HYMN.

THE spirit that within me dwells
    Tells me truly of a love divine;
An inward monitor surely tells
    A hopeful truth that Heaven is mine.

Though sick'ning sorrow may appall,
    My soul awhile may be cast down,
Yet if I in prayer on God will call,
    Sweet peace will all my efforts crown.

For God is love, and my prayer doth soar
    To Him, and I ne'er implore in vain;
And though beset 'midst breakers' roar,
    He'll take me safe to shore again.

His promise He will most surely keep ;
  My soul trusts to His graciousness,
For there is a time to laugh, as well to weep,
  And all good men's actions He will bless.

My spirit longs to soar to heaven's space,
  Those realms beyond the azure sky.
Lord, I would seek Thy pardoning grace,
  As to Thy breast I fain would fly.

I shall ever trust Thee, Lord of heaven,
  As by Thy Son our grace is wrought ;
By His blood I hope to be forgiven ;
  Salvation by His death was bought.

HYMN.

FAIN would we fly to Thee, O God,
  Our Father and our Friend,
So Thou couldst instil Thy sacred word,
  And succor to us send.

The cares of the world now weigh us down,
  The load is hard to bear,
We reap the fruits of sin deep sown,
  Which won our heart-strings tear.

Thy laws, O God, if disobeyed,
    Brings their own punishment sure,
And all Thy power is then arrayed
    To scourge the evil doer.

We long to dwell in Thy sweet realm,
    Where we Thy grace could find.
O steer us with Thy guiding helm,
    To leave our sins behind !

HYMN.

Our souls shall not in oblivion lie,
    When our mortal frames are dead,
For from the cross there came a cry,
    When Jesus bowed His head.

That cry went forth to heaven high,
    That believers might still live;
We know His holy spirit is nigh,
    Our confessions to receive.

Good Lord, we now confess to Thee,
    In humility and shame,
For we turned our eyes to iniquity,
    And hallowed not Thy name.

But Thou art merciful and just,
   And for Thy grace we plead ;
In Thy charity we put our trust,
   To help us in our need.

Rake out our souls from oblivion's dust,
   Lift out our spirits sure,
Soften our hearts' dull hardened crust,
   Make us refined and pure.

And when Thou callst from yonder height,
   May we listen to Thy voice,
Redeemed conquerors in life's fight,
   May we become Thy choice.

HYMN.

GLORY to Thee, my God in Heaven,
   Who rulest the universe with power ;
To us Thou hast most freely given
   This earthly sphere as a precious dower.

May we tend it with due care
   Acceptable to Thy holy sight ;
For we of Thy great bounties share
   When Thou bringest to view scenes of delight.

Nature is arrayed in emerald hue
   To gladden our senses and please our minds ;
Each day Thou dost the scene renew,
   And garlands of beauty Thy love binds.

The starry heavens Thy power do show,
   The seas and mountains colossal rise ;
Where'er we turn, where'er we go,
   Thy exalted works do us surprise.

HYMN.

Hark ! I hear yond tolling bell
   Calling sinners to God's throne,
From craggy mountain, plain, and dell,
   Sounding with a heaven-like tone.

Yes, it calleth to the sinners
   To bear in mind the acts they've done,
If they heed it, they will be winners,
   And reach the home that Jesus won.

Aye! He won it by His blood,
   Nail'd like a felon to the tree,
Whilst round Him weeping sisters stood
   Crying, "Lord we hope in Thee."

Yond bell is tolling for the upright,
  So they steadfast can remain ;
It seems to say that Heaven's in sight,
  And men's worship is not in vain.

The solemn tones of yonder bell
  To children's tender minds will bring
The hope of Heaven or the fear of hell,
  And make their budding sins take wing.

The cadence of the last stroke given
  Still lingers on our list'ning ears,
And like the music of sweet Heaven
  It cheers our fast declining years.

HYMN.

Lord, fit us for Thy realms above,
  Heavenly mansions Thou hast made ;
Extend to us Thy holy love,
  O leave us not in benighted shade !

And when in that celestial
  Our ethereal spirits soar in joy,
Do Thou gently lead us by Thy hand
  Where no earthly sins annoy.

Grant we may sing in joyous tone,
　And homage offer unto Thee,
Where the lamps of life have e'er shone
　From beginning of eternity.

May we greet the angelic race,
　Those *now* winged cherubs of olden times,
Whose history we've loved to trace,
　And with them offer our sweetest chimes.

Hallelujah, hallelujah, to Thee above!
　And forever be Thy glorious name!
O give us faith in Thy holy love,
　And keep us from backsliding shame.

———

HYMN.

GLORY be to Thee, my God,
　My everlasting King;
Thou wert where'er I trod,
　With angels on the wing.

Glory and honor to Thy name,
　My Father to Thee I sing;
Keep me always from sin's blame.
　That my conscience ne'er may sting.

Glory and power be to Thee,
  Supreme Judge in realms above,
For all our actions Thou canst see,
  And canst cheer us with Thy love.

Glory and peace we offer now,
  In humility we pray;
To Thy name we lowly bow,
  O take us from sin away!

Glory and homage are ever due
  To Thee in heaven above;
For thy mercy we now sue,
  Ever trusting to Thy love.

HYMN.

We know there is a God supreme,
  For His marvellous works we see;
It surely is not a passing dream
  That we mark them on land and sea.

Our senses cannot so far stray
  That we heed not His blessings here,
For He dispenses night and day
  His charity and kind cheer.

From youth to age He mercy pours
  On every one that is born,
And watches o'er our childhood's hours
  So that we should not be forlorn.

He reigns above the stormy cloud,
  And his eyes are o'er us cast ;
No obstacle His eye can shroud
  In the present or the past.

O yes, there is a God of grace,
  Most bountiful and just,
And all of us will see his face
  That in Him put our trust.

Teach us and lead us to Thy throne,
  Above the ethereal sky,
That when we leave this earthly zone.
  Hosannas we may cry.

HYMN.

If I should ever separated be
  From my dearest friends so kind,
O God, wouldst Thou draw near to me.
  And I ever Thy kind favor find !

May the Comforter descend to my soul,
   And cheer all my exiled days,
And like the magnet pointing to the pole,
   Keep true and steady to me always.

May Thy holy presence e'er watch o'er me,
   As in distant realms I stray around ;
May Thy guiding shadow go before me,
   And my footsteps follow it on the ground.

Lord, be near me, awake or sleeping,
   Be Thou my guide for evermore !
And as thy hour-glass our time is keeping,
   Fit me for Thy glorious shore.

Let me trust Thee, O great Father !
   Grant my safety to secure ;
For I know that Thou wouldst rather
   That we should no cares endure.

And when it pleases Thee to gather
   The wanderer to his loving friends,
May I remember, Heavenly Father,
   Consolation to man Thou lovingly sends.

HYMN.

STEER me clear from tempting sin,
Lord, let me Thy temple enter in !
Let me in there to reign in peace,
Grant to my soul a Heavenly lease !
Lead me not into the deep quagmire,
To Thee I tune my fervent lyre,
To Thee in praise I joyful sing,
My God, my all, my sacred King.
Shield me in my weakness here,
Drive from my soul every fear,
Strengthen me with Thy holy love,
And fit me for Thy courts above.
Thou sent Messiah my soul to save,
And to lead me o'er the land and wave ;
Instil into my heart Thy word,
And make me know Thou art the Lord.
And when I die, O save my soul,
By Christ inscribed on Thy holy roll !
Praise and hallelujah now I sing,
To great Jehovah and holy King.

HYMN.

I AM cheered by the ray of light
    That beams within my soul ;
My breast is filled with fond delight,
    For my Saviour made me whole.

Gladly I sing this song of praise,
    And my soul no remorse feels,
To the Father my voice I raise,
    For he all my sorrow heals.

Unchained from sinful course I stand,
    With no brand of vicious stain ;
God's Word is read in every land
    That all souls may Heaven gain.

What comfort, Lord, we all derive
    From out Thy words of grace !
It is Thy will none to deprive
    From seeing Thy hallowed face.

Whilst I have got a spark of life,
    I'll obey Thee most sincerely,
Like Abraham with uplifted knife,
    Show that I do love Thee dearly.

HYMN.

To Thee, my God, I offer praise,
    As devoutly here I stand ;
Thou knowest all my sinful ways,
    For they're countless as the sand.

I bow in heartfelt sorrow now
    To Thee, my God, in Heaven,
And feel in spirit lone and low,
    And pray to be forgiven.

O tenderly on me look down
    From off Thy Throne of grace,
And me, Thy child, do not disown,
    Because I turned from Thy face.

I've followed Satan's footsteps oft,
    And trod where he has been,
Now, Lord, I cast mine eyes aloft,
    And henceforth on Thee I lean.

HYMN.

SACRED tunes we sing, hosannas now we cry,
To Thee, O God, above, we in repentance sigh !
Stung by grievous sins our consciences do not approve,
We lift our voices towards Heaven, trusting in Thy love.

We're prone to do wrong, and now supplicate Thy grace.
Turn not away from us thy sanctified face !
But listen to our prayers, also our humble praise,
As we to Thee tremulously our lowly voices raise.

And what is man that Thou shouldst e'er for him care?
Naught but a mortal being who cruel torments bear.
His life is but a span of woes, dire discord and disease,
And only at Thy footstool can his soul find any ease.

So we kneel down in adoration of Thy kingly name,
Asking for Thy blessing, as by Thy mandate here we
    came ;
Thou madest us in Thine image, so forgive us ere we
    die,
As we to Thy throne of grace in humility draw nigh.

Thou sent Thy Son from Heaven to save us from sins,
And all them who trust in Him a home in paradise wins.
Show us the path to tread, the straight and narrow road.
Our sins to leave behind so our consciences ne'er to
    goad.

And when our earthly race is run, hosanna's may we
    sing
To Thee, our God in Heaven, our great and glorious
    King,

With angels for companions who sing to Thee in
   Heaven,
Waving flags of peace and chanting, "Our sins are now
   forgiven."

HYMN.

(MISSIONARY.)

How scattered are the Lord's flock !
   In zealous bands they love to roam ;
Though sprung from a saintly stock,
   Yet some are far away from home.

Far away in distant lands they spread
   The tidings of a Saviour's love
To them whose souls have ne'er been led
   To know there is a God above.

They work in a vineyard where fruit is green ;
   Hard toil is theirs that must be done ;
They see many a revolting scene
   Before the truimphal crown is won.

This scattered flock are duly working
   For the salvation of human kind ;
In those benighted lands there is no shirking,
   But the bond of brotherhood they bind.

Boldly must they face fatigue,
   Oft dangers menace in front and rear ;
But with their God they are in league,
   So forth they march devoid of fear.

Malarious fevers spread in their camp,
   Beasts of prey lurk round at night,
And oft they hear the hostile tramp
   Of treacherous foes that come to fight.

And when toilsome martyrdom is o'er,
   Sickly and feeble some return to die,
Alas ! some are laid in a foreign shore
   Whose spirits God hath ta'en on high.

HYMN.

Guide us, Lord, with Thy right hand
   When treacherous foes are lurking round
Unseen by us, yet Thou canst wave Thy wand
   To the place where vilest sinners abound.

Framed in falsehood, beset by human power,
   Deceitful men lie in wait for our souls ;
Lord, thou canst make their standing lower,
   As swiftly as this globe in its orbit rolls.

Puffed up by pride and vain conceit,
   Arrayed in gorgeous outside dress,
Alas ! they know not Thy mercy's seat,
   But are given to great ungodliness.

From such, O Lord, let us turn aside,
   And list not to their vile discourse;
For all is deception where such abide,
   From whence corruption hath its source.

Lead us away from sin and darkness,
   Lest we should go astray from Thee,
For better is solitude with bitter loneliness,
   Than for us to turn from Thy decree.

Lord cheer us all as through life we go,
   Journeying on to man's last estate ;
Life hath its trials and death brings woe,
   But patiently on Thee we will wait.

Chorus—Glory ! glory be to Thee,
         God our Father and our friend,
         Who from Thy great eternity
         Will succor to the needy send.

HYMN.

(FUNERAL.)

Lo ! our dear sister sleepeth
  Locked in her Saviour's arms,
Alas ! her kindred weepeth,
  For death hath took her charms.

But she is now an angel pure,
  And resting up in heaven,
There her soul hath found a cure,
  For God took what He had given.

He took her spirit that did dwell
  Encased in a mortal's frame ;
We know that He doeth all things well,
  For to her sweet Jesus came.

He whisper'd to her words of grace,
  And told of His Father's love,
Then with beaming halo on His face
  He took her to joys above.

Cease weeping, sisters, O pray cease,
  And mourn not any more,
Our sister's soul hath found release,
  And dwells on Jordan's shore.

Now we'll pray that God will take
  Compassion on all here,
And for the blessed Jesus' sake
  We'll pray beside her bier.

HYMN FOR CHRISTMAS.

JOSEPH and Mary had to flee
  And leave their friends behind,
Before the Wise Men came to see
  The Saviour of mankind.

The Star of Bethlehem shone that day
  The Son of God was born,
As in the manger He did lay,
  The Virgin mother quite forlorn.

'Tis the anniversary of the birth
  Of Him who took our sins away,
Salvation is granted o'er this earth,
  No matter what disbelievers say;

For when their time of death draws near
  At the eleventh hour they call
(When they are filled with mortal fear),
  "Jesus have mercy on my soul!"

HYMN.

WE'RE from pestilence and famine free,
And bless'd with health, O Lord, from **Thee**;
How happy ought our lot to be,
If we obey our God's decree.

Healthful breezes fan every cheek,
Of them that would thy favor seek;
Humbly we thank **Thee** in accents **meek,**
For Thou'rt the defender of the weak.

No scourge oppresses, for here we stand,
As marks of Thy all-powerful hand;
Grant us **a place in** Thy seraph band
That sings to Thee in Heaven's land.

We praise Thee for Thy goodness now,
To Thee in thankfulness we bow,
Within us rises a fervent glow
Of love for all Thou dost bestow.

HYMN.

WHEN thoughts of guilt bow down my soul,
  My God, I turn to Thee;
For, Lord, I'm like a horrid ghoul,
  That should from dark ways flee.

Despondency o'er my spirit steals,
  Deep is my conscience seared,
My heart great inward sorrow feels,
  By me Thy wrath is feared.

What is man that Thou mindful art,
  And ministerest to his desires?
Thou knowledge doth to him impart,
  To quench unholy fires.

Born in weakness, but in Thy power,
  I appeal to Thee for grace ;
O let me hide in Thy holy tower,
  And win the heavenly race.

HYMN.

Lord guide me from the enemy waiting
  My soul to slay with deadly sin,
Fain would I the wicked be hating,
  To keep old Satan from entering in.

Teach me to shun the baited trap.
  That would my wandering feet decoy,
So I can avoid the dread mishap
  That seeks my soul to destroy.

Lead me with Thy holy zeal
   Which Thou oft our Fathers be show'd,
For Beelzebub my soul would steal,
   And my doomed spirit bow'd.

Keep me from wretched dark despair,
   And take me under Thy wing,
That my spirit may be light as air,
   And to Thy great glory sing.

HYMN.

We'll cross the river of Jordan soon,
   And reach the other shore,
Where trees will cast their shade at noon,
   When we are ferried o'er.

Shaded forever will be our sins,
   No burning pangs we'll feel ;
For all the sinners that Jordan wins,
   The goodly waters heal.

In the city we'll find shelter good,
   To shield from sin and shame ;
Refresh'd we'll rise from the cleansing flood ;
   And call on Jehovah's name.

'Tis a refuge for the weary souls,
　　Who have been careworn with pain,
And as o'er them the water rolls,
　　It will wash away each stain.

HYMN.

(FOR SEAMEN).

WHEN tempest-tost on ocean's wave,
　　We see God's power above ;
He nerves the seamen to be brave,
　　And guards them with His love.

Grand and sublime the ocean rolls ;
　　How dark and weird the sky !
The rolling waves with crested scrolls,
　　Yet good sailors them defy.

Reared and trained to duty's law,
　　First to their *God*, then *man*,
The vessel may be pooped or yaw,
　　Yet they ken the nautical plan.

A wave may burst on frailest deck,
　　A spar perhaps carried away,
Perchance the ship become a wreck,
　　Yet, through God, they ne'er dismay.

So roll on, ye breakers, roll on apace,
  As windy cyclones blow ;
Pious seamen will God's chart trace,
  The sacred book aloft and alow.

HYMN.

I THANK Thee, Lord, for favors sent,
  Presented by Thy hand above ;
For when my earthly hopes are spent
  Thou sendest me sweet heavenly love.

For who so great as Thee, my God,
  Who comprehendest all,
And cheers me by Thy sacred word,
  And lifts me whene'er I fall.

I feel, Lord, that I should grateful be
  For all gifts enjoyed here,
And now upon my bended knee
  My soul to Thee draws near.

I praise Thee in Thy holy place,
  The place not made with hands,
O grant that I the track may trace,
  Where reign the seraph bands.

HYMN.

THERE is a spring from which I love to drink ;
    The water flows free for all to take ;
And whene'er my spirits downward sink,
    My thirst from that fountain I oft slake.

Refresh'd I rise a frowning world to meet;
    New life is infused into my soul ;
I humbly kneel at God's mercy seat,
    And drink from the spring on Calvary's knoll.

Could all vile sinners know the good
    That emanates from yonder spring !
'Tis where our Saviour oft hath stood
    When pilgrims did rich offerings bring.

That fountain ne'er dries up at all :
    The purest crystal waters run,
And when I obey the gospel's call,
    It sounds the knell that Heaven is won.

HYMN.

I'll take my " title deeds," into the courts above,
And plead before the Judge of divinity and love ;
I'll say that wiser men than me the documents have
      made
And a right to salvation by them is surely made.

The sceptics to my "title deeds" will wonder at the
    sight,
When they find what seems a mystery is so clear and
    right.
The interpreters of old were wiser than they think,
For the records of the disciples then were just from the
    ink.
And after Christianity has stood thro' long ages past,
'Tis more likely by our modern thought it will forever
    last.
My "title deeds" give me a heritage in lands beyond
    the sky,
Where I hope to meet the present sceptics convinced by
    and by;
But it will only be by getting "title deeds" now be-
    fore they start.
Which can be had for asking, and a regenerated heart.
The "title deeds" are warrantee, and never known to
    fail,
And can be gotten by the felon in the loathsome prison
    jail;
But he must strike the shackles off that bind his soul
    to sin,
Or else he never can the fold of good Heaven enter in.
The rich man of the earth also can "title deeds" obtain.
If he will from pride of heart and from sinful lusts
    abstain.

And in charity to the **poor** folks, by alms freely given,

Though he cannot **go** through a needle's eye, he can
the gates of Heaven.

The convocation of the learned men have ordained the
decree

By the ancient scrip before the inauguration of the **Holy**
See.

And what was theirs to trust to in faith shall ever be
my creed,

That is to love **my God** above, and help a brother in
need.

Then when the trumpet sounds the **Judge above** will
say :

"By the 'title deeds' **you** held so **firm you have surely**
won the day."

HYMN.

No man can serve two masters here ;
  The choice to us is given,
And all that would from Satan steer,
  Must obey the Lord in Heaven.

But they that want to Sheol go
  Can follow Satan's wiles,
For he will lead to sin and woe
  With artful crafty smiles.

He lays in wait for every chance
 To prey upon mankind ;
You'll find him in the ball-room dance,
 When folks are giddy blind.

But the Lord is ever nigh to all,
 That are perplexed sore,
And if we on His name will call,
 He will compassion pour.

And if we've let Satan in before,
 And then repent sincerely,
He'll drive him out at open door,
 And love us ever dearly.

Now we'll sing in glee once more,
 And one Master only serve,
We'll serve Him till we reach His shore
 Nor from His will e'er swerve.

HYMN.

Peace, perfect peace, bestowed by God on high !
Here no tears are shed, and hush'd is every sigh.
Our hearts are light and free, no sin doth enter here,
For we have a Saviour's love our spirits e'er to cheer.

Peace, perfect peace, ever reigneth here supreme ;
Our souls are happy now as in ecstatic dream,
For we know no sorrow, and we're free from pain,
And we'll sing to God above a sweet joyful strain.

Peace, perfect peace, Jesus conquered for all,
When to His Father above from the cross he did call.
The sins of mankind were then all forgiven,
When He paved the true way to His Father in heaven.

Peace, perfect peace, 'till to the tomb we all go ;
When our souls are in Paradise, God's angels will show
Those places of peace and delight evermore,
When we reach the precincts of the heavenly shore.

Peace, perfect peace, in loving brotherhood,
With angelic sisters, and our dear brothers good,
We'll stray in that happy land united once more,
And our voices in harmony, we'll Jehovah adore.

Peace, perfect peace, for the nations all round,
When the blasts of the bugle charge will never more
      sound ;
The swords shall be rusted, and the forts all decay,
When the Lord ushers in the Millennium day.

Peace, perfect peace, hosannas we'll sing,
To the great Lord of Heaven, our meek peaceful King,

Whose majesty and power are ever sublime,
Whom the nations have worship'd, from beginning of
time.

Peace, perfect peace, to the heathens away,
Far in the jungle from gospel's bright ray !
The olive branch we'll carry far o'er the blue sea,
To bring Thy dear children, O Lord, unto Thee.

HYMN.

HARK I hear the *herald's* blast,
   Proclaiming that Jesus died,
So sinners in Sheol should not be cast
   If they become purified.

A prescription He has made out
   To heal my soul from sin,
And loving angels loud will shout
   When God's Kindgom I go in.

The remedy what His *heralds* proclaim
   And in sorrow weep for me,
Is that I should call on His holy name,
   And lowly bend my knee.

My prayer and praise I'll to Him give,
    And humbly sue for grace ;
Then I will a pardon surely receive,
    And my trangressions He'll efface.

And then His herald will forth steer
    To spread the news around,
And make it plainly to appear
    A clean conscience I have found.

Rejoiced will be my brethren's souls
    When God's herald doth so procl iim ;
Far o'er the plains and mountain knolls
    Will be heard Messiah's name.

HYMN.

(BETHEL.)

WE'LL dry our cups, and drink no more,
But head our bark for Jordan's shore.
With Christ at the helm we have no fear,
For our Saviour knoweth where to steer.

Tho' rocks and shoals beset our way,
Yet from a true course He will not stray ;
He is the Captain of a crew of braves,
And no more we'll be old Satan's slaves.

Before the wind we'll run with flowing sheet,
And our old ship-mates in port we'll meet ;
We'll clear the decks, and for action clear,
If Satan's imps should for us steer.

A broadside we'll pour into their side,
And triumphant on the gospel ride ;
We'll give three cheers for Captain Christ
And the flag of salvation to the peak will hoist.

HYMN.

CONSECRATE my heart, O God,
   And sanctify my soul,
As I travel on earth's road
   Or where the waves do roll.

Purify me with Thy grace ;
   Bestow on me Thy love,
That I a sinful world may face,
   And grant me peace above.

Let old things pass away,
   And new ones come instead,
That brighter may be each day
   Which passes o'er my head.

Lord, have compassion now,
 As I'm kneeling at Thy feet,
Implant upon my aching brow
 The stamp of pardon from Thy seat.

HYMN.

(MISSIONARY.)

YES, in the field the harvesters are at their goodly work,
They are cutting swaths of sin from the Pagan and the
 Turk.
They cut close to the ground the vile and stubborn
 frail,
So that the influence of Pagan priests never more will
 prevail.
Mahomet's power is now a myth all in the Moslem
 world,
And the South-Sea idols are in the briny deep forever
 hurl'd;
Now all their rites and ceremonies are as an idle dream,
And no more will weeping widows drown in Ganges
 far off stream.
No more will Buddhist priests the souls of men destroy,
For now the good evangelists their harvest-men deploy,
The Caffre shall lie down in peace, with no fear of
 dread

Of priestly orders given to cut off his benighted head.

Afric's children bloody sacrifices never more will see,

For the harvesters are dispensing the gospel true and
    free.

No more shall the Maori to cannibalism be given,

For the harvesters will give him hallow'd food from
    Heaven.

No more shall the war-whoop sound and scalping
    knives be used,

And the frontier pale-face woman by miscreants be
    abused ;

For the harvesters have ta'en the camp of roguery and
    sin,

And with their sickles cut a road to let the Bible in.

No more shall the Esquimaux in rude barbarism roam,

In yonder frigid region where he makes his frozen home,

He shall be clothed with righteousness and our Saviour's
    love

To fit him for the heavenly mansions in regions high
    above.

Yes, the harvesters are reaping a rich reward most sure,

And they have the spirit all hardships to cheerily en-
    dure :

And when their work is done the Lord will to them
    say,

" Come ye, enter in my vineyard to rest each night
    and day."

HYMN.

(FOR A CHILD.)

O LORD, I rise from my little bed,
   And I know you did me wake ;
In your good book 'tis surely said
   You'll love me for Jesus' sake.

Suffer a little child to come to you,
   And hear my morning prayer.
Now Lord to you I humbly sue
   For in Heaven you are there.

Spare my father and my mother,
   And your goodness I will tell ;
Love my sister and my brother,
   For I love them all so well.

If e'er I'm naughty and sulky grow,
   Let me rude manners ever mend ;
Lord, to you I kneel and bow,
   For you are my heavenly friend.

You sent sweet Jesus for us all ;
   He'll love me when I do right ;
Lord, let your blessings on me fall
   Every morning until night.

HYMN.

WHEN restless on my bed I lay,
  And my fevered lips are sore,
A prayer to God I humbly say,
  And to Him my sorrows pour.

He straightway then dispels my pain,
  And all my sorrows quickly vanish,
And soon my normal strength regain,
  And sickly sufferings banish.

Then with bright eyes and nerves more strong,
  And heart in a grateful mood,
To God I turn my thankful song,
  And praise Him for his good.

My sleep is sound ; refresh'd I rise ;
  No ills surround to grieve.
The vilest sinners He'll not despise,
  But will their prayers receive.

How joyful it is then for me
  To acknowledge His great boon ;
He makes my spirit light and free,
  Fift and soonor His aid came swift and soon.

Holy, holy, Lord above !
  I praise Thy name on earth ;
Thou show'd to man Thy holy love,
  By the gentle Jesus' birth.

HYMN.

Lord, lead me to Thy courts of Zion,
For Thy word I will ever rely on ;
Lead me where Thy cherubims sing
Who to Thee sweet off'rings bring.

Lead me, tho' in sin I am sunk,
And oft from Satan's bowl have drunk ;
Lead me by Thy gracious hand,
To stroll in Zion's happy land.

Lead me to loved ones gone before me,
Who in Heaven now adore Thee ;
Lead me from dark woes and sorrow,
So I may Christ's footsteps follow.

Lead me to Thy footstool above,
God of mercy, and God of love ;
Lead me where Thou dost abide,
And forever be my only guide.

HYMN.

Lo ! from the clouds I hear a voice,
   Calling for God's faithful tribes,
To whom He gave a loving choice
   To study the inspired scribes.

Let me be Thy choice, and give me aid
   To read Thy holy prophets of old ;
To understand the pages Thou hast made,
   To lead me to Thy secure fold.

When weary of heart to them I turn,
   And consolation I'm sure to find ;
I rise impress'd, for there I learn,
   To love my God and fellow-kind.

May I dwell in peace for evermore
   In shadow of Thy holy wing,
And as a duty Thee adore,
   As to the cross I fondly cling.

HYMN.

Almighty God, who hast revealed the end of man,
   For the olden prophets through Thee have said
That in Thy divine wisdom Thou didst plan
   The glorious resurrection of the dead.

And when man's power beginneth to fail,
  Thou ever interposeth to make him strong ;
Thine ear is attentive to list to tender tale,
  And loveth to hear the penitential song.

Lord, fit us for Thy presence when we arise
  From the dark grave when the seventh trumpet blows.
Let ministering angels attend us to the skies,
  When Christ under footstool tramples on His foes.

The angel said, "That time should be no longer,
  But all the kingdoms here should be Thine for ever-
    more."
We beseech that we in faith become more stronger
  So that we may live on thy celestial shore.

HYMN.

Why should we pine when God is good,
  To give us all we need below ?
For Jesus shed his precious blood,
  And seeds of blessings He did sow.

In vain regrets our lives are past,
  'Tis time ill spent if we would think ;
On Jesus let our hopes be cast,
  And never let our spirits sink.

When dark despair our senses steal,
  And nerveless is our body's frame,
Oh, Jesus can our sorrows heal,
  If we call upon his Holy name,

He loveth not to chide us here,
  He wishes all His children well;
He can banish all our fear,
  And vain pining can dispel.

He can our souls to joy soon bring;
  He can lift our hearts on high,
If we to Him our praises sing,
  And in our prayers humbly cry,

HYMN.

We reverence Thee, O God on high,
  As supreme Judge of this vile earth;
Our souls to Thee will now draw nigh,
  And worship Thee of heavenly worth.

Thou delightest not in sacrifice alone,
  But that we should obey Thy will;
Thy great compassion to us shone,
  When Jesus died on Calvary's hill.

For grace and guidance, Lord, we cry
  To Thee who sits on holy throne;
Hear our voices in repentance sigh,
  And lowly and sin-stricken is the tone.

Cast us not away from Thy omniscient sight!
  Shield us with Thy heavenly love !
Lord, we praise Thee day and night,
  Hoping to reach thy home above.

HYMN.

(TUNE, "Greenland's Icy Mountains.")

FROM Umpqua's verdant mountains,
  From Coos Bay's glist'ning strand.
From Cascade's rushing fountains,
  To Clatsop's far-famed land,
Is told the ancient story
  Of how the Saviour died,
Which fills our souls with glory,
  When He was crucified.

Come, come, ye sinners hoary,
  And listen to this theme,
Of spikes and spears so gory,
  With blood flowing astream.

Waft, Chinook winds, the story,
  For His saints good tidings bring,
Of Him who died in **glory**,
  Immanuel, God and King.

Bring here the lamp of brightness
  That shines in every soul ;
The young, the ag'd and sightless,
  For faith can make them whole.

Tell the Indians of nature,
  That Messiah has them saved;
He died for every creature,
  And the road to Heaven paved.

HYMN.

THY ways, O Lord, are not our ways,
  For we know Thou art divine ;
As on Thy wondrous works we gaze,
  We see beauty in each line.

Thy ways, so different from earthly man,
  In wisdom exalted shine,
We note the great universe's plan,
  That whirls through endless time.

How grand Thy Heavens in boundless space,
　　All so dazzling to behold !
And the planets in their annual race,
　　Thy glorious works unfold.

How vast the spheres that eternal roll !
　　Even our globe where seasons change,
And man himself with ethereal soul,
　　Thou mad'st the earth to range.

Thy holy word Thou gavest to him,
　　For his comfort and his guide ;
That gift in memory can ne'er be dim,
　　For Thou art always by his side,

Thy ways omnipotent are strange,
　　To the feeble mind of man,
Thy omniscient eye takes lofty range,
　　Our transgressions e'er to scan.

HYMN.

We're going to the New Jerusalem,
　　To the mansions of the blest ;
'Tis there we'll fondly hail them
　　That have gone to eternal rest.

'Tis there we'll stray in glory
　　All through the paths of Heaven,
And tell our friends the story
　　That God hath us forgiven.

We'll sing angelic anthems
　　To God upon His throne,
And wear a crown of diadems
　　Gathered in the heavenly zone.

There we'll meet but never part,
　　But be linked in love's bright chain,
When gladness will fill each heart,
　　And vanished be all our pain.

Our praises will sound in boundless space,
　　Which to God will echo loud;
And there we'll see our Saviour's face
　　Amongst the angelic crowd.

We are bound for yonder holy site,
　　Where sorrow flees away,
And they that gave "The widow's mite."
　　Shall in bliss forever stay.

HYMN.

THERE is a land we all would like to win,
    And enter in the portals of a heavenly sphere ;
Where no false heart of man can ever enter in,
    And where God preserves his loving children dear.

It is an abode of eternal bliss so goodly pure,
    Where the cherubim roam in everlasting delight,
And aching hearts of men have found a sure cure,
    A balm for every wound, redeemed by God's might.

A land of great purity unstained by worldly sin,
    Where chants the congregation of the holy saints.
All that are truly penitent can freely enter in,
    Where cordiality and love in forgiveness them awaits.

O let us henceforth try a godly life to lead,
    That yonder fair haven we may at last all reach,
Where angel kindred are gone whose hearts here did
      bleed,
    Who'll show us the paths of Heaven and the will of
      God can teach.

There we'll see our Creator who knew us from our
      birth,
    Sitting on His throne, passing judgment on us all ;
For in His book is registered the sins we've done on
      earth,
    And the names of the *just spirits* heavenly angels call.

O Lord, wilt Thou have mercy and lead us to Thy stand;
  Take us to the regions of celestial holy light;
Take us, Thy dear children, and lead us by Thy hand,
  From this darksome world to Thy kingdom pure and
    bright.

HYMN.

A PRODIGAL I return from wandering
  To my Father, who looks with strained eyes;
To waywardness my soul is ever pandering;
  For my return my anxious Father sighs.

I'll fall at His feet and penitent will cry
  "O Father forgive Thy wilful son before Thee,
And do Thou my soul forever sanctify,
  And in pity grant sweet succor unto me!"

My Father me then tenderly will raise,
  And clasp me to his holy bosom warm;
Alas! He knoweth my prodigal wasteful ways,
  For all my sufferings He'll find a healing balm.

He'll give me blessings from sweet Heaven;
  He'll grant me the joys of this earth in store;
He'll say in his mercy I'm freely forgiven,
  As we fondly embrace to part no more.

I'll offer praises to him and ever sweetly sing,
  In chorus with the angels at his shrine,
As to his footstool I sorrowfully bring
  My wandering feet from a foreign clime.

While angels sing their anthems of great glee,
  The cherubim will fly around with radiant love;
A seat by His side my Father will give to me,
  At his love-feast in courts of joy above.

HYMN.

AND shall I see my Saviour's face,
  When I leave this world of woe?
Shall I be redeemed by His grace?
  And shall I to Heaven go?

I hope sincerely to merit His smile,
  And have all my sins forgiven;
Then I'll be freed from worldly guile,
  And enter the gates of Heaven.

I'll seek Him while He may be found,
  And worship at His throne;
Then my heart will be made sound,
  And of more exalted tone.

Prone as I am to wander away,
   From paths of virtue bright,
Lord, let me not e'er go astray,
   But keep me in Thy sight.

HYMN.

LORD, give me strength of mind and heart,
   To withstand sin's alluring ways,
That I may steer clear of Satan's dart,
   And be happy all my days.

I'm prone to turn aside from Thee,
   And apt from Thy commands to stray ;
To Thy bosom I fain would flee,
   To be blest by angelic ray.

Prostrate I pray at Thy shrine,
   And now in penitence I crave,
O let Thy angels now combine
   To succor in need a sinful slave !

In hope I turn my pleading eye
   Heavenward to implore Thy aid ;
Lord, heal my soul before I die,
   And I be laid in the darkly shade !

HYMN.

LORD grant our correspondence with Thee may lead
   To blessings of purest grace,
And that the sown grain of mustard seed
   Be means to lead us to Thy face ;

And that our words and acts correspond,
   And never to backslide from Thee,
So that our spirits ne'er should despond,
   But we should ever cheerful be.

When we're depressed by vain desires,
   O let Thy spirit give us hope !
Quench the withering and blasting fires,
   When in blind sin we ever grope ;

And ake us with our sinful loads
   To Thy throne so spotless white ;
Cleanse our souls by Thy sacred codes
   That makes the sinners pure and bright.

Lord, our trust is in Thy goodness now,
   To redeem us evermore ;
To Thy holy will we humbly bow,
   And Thy name we all adore.

In contrition our sins we feel,
   We ask Thy aid to set us free ;
At Thy footstool we humbly kneel,
   And rest our hopes of peace on Thee.

HYMN.

I THANK Thee, Lord, for favors sent,
  They are from Thy hand above ;
For when my earthly hopes are spent,
  Thou sendst Heavenly love.

For who so great as Thee my God,
  Who comprehendest all,
And cheers me by Thy sacred word
  And lifts me when I fall ?

Lord, how grateful I should be
  For all gifts bestowed here ;
And now, upon my bended knee,
  My soul to Thee draws near.

I praise Thee in Thy holy place,
  The place not made with hands,
O grant that I the track may trace,
  To join the angel bands !

HYMN.

Lo ! the Saviour's presence is round us ;
  We feel His influence, and grace ;
Though sinners here, His love hath found us,
  For His spirit pervades all space.

Like a magnet He's attractive,
  Closely twining round our hearts ;
His omniscient eye is ever active,
  Searching out our hidden parts.

Though we falter, yet He is near ;
  Though we go astray, He'll find,
Though we weep, He'll dry the tear ;
  Though sin-fetter'd, He'll unbind.

Precious Saviour, we humbly crave Thee,
  That Thou wouldst chase our sins away ;
For we adore Thy Father, who gave Thee,
  For our sakes, at crucifixion day.

HYMN.

GRATEFUL PRAISES.

I have a solace in Jesus' love,
  More precious than rubies fine ;
That consolation comes from above,
  'Tis hallowed and divine.

What would be life without its aid,
  To cheer me on the way ?
'Twould be like a cheerless shade
  Without a sunny ray.

But gratitude I'll show to Him
   For all His love to me ;
As age creeps on my eyes grow dim,
   Yet I will thankful be.

His love for me hath oft been shown
   On stormy sea and land,
When in despair and hope had flown
   I've felt His saving hand.

When battle raged midst deadly foes,
   His presence shielded me ;
When sick and near unto death's throes,
   He set me from ailments free.

When storms have dash'd my gallant barque,
   Like the flotsam on the wave,
His outstretch'd arm at midnight dark,
   Hath been the One to save.

And when perplex'd by fellow man
   Perverse in all his ways,
O, God, Thou thwarted his sinful plan,
   And vexed sore his days.

For Thy mercies vouchsafed to me
   In gratitude I sing,
To Thee in Thy eternity,
   My Saviour and my King.

HYMN.

WE praise Thee, O Jehovah great,
That rules over every nation's fate;
Thy great power supremely stands
In celestial and terrestrial lands.

From chaos Thou framed this earthly sphere,
To Thee we owe our inheritance here;
Without Thy aid we would as nothing be,
So we offer our sincere praise to Thee.

Let our prayers ascend to Thine holy ear,
Grant us Thy favor from year to year;
And as time rolls on, guide us aright,
Keep us ever in Thy holy sight.

Lord, when we leave this vale of sin,
Grant heavenly precincts we may win;
To reign with Thee to endless time,
In Thy celestial home sublime.

Let us see faces of loved ones gone,
Whose kind spirits left us here forlorn;
Lord, join us together once more in love,
To live in harmony and peace above.

To part no more!   To part no more!
But dwell together on Jordan's shore ;
To part no more!   But live with Thee,
O, God, in great immensity !

HYMN.

LORD, when I give unto the poor
    I'm lending unto Thee ;
In charity when I ope my door,
    I make sad sorrow flee.

And when distress I see around
    'Tis pleasure then to give;
When the poor a friend hath found,
    Their blessings I receive.

Thy bounties, Lord, to me are great
    So I will dispense in joy
A part of my worldly estate,
    Then 'tis pleasure without alloy.

If sinners come and ask a share,
    I will to them all dispense,
For well I know that Thou wilt care
    When my soul shall go from hence.

Lord, I'll make no distinction here,
  As Thou dost not up in Heaven ;
For sinners here have naught to fear
  As by Christ we're all forgiven.

If we will turn from our ways,
  And hallow God's holy name,
He will accept our sincere praise,
  And free us from sin and shame.

HYMN.

GLORY be to my Saviour dear,
  In memory of His name !
For by His blood my soul is clear,
  By Him redemption came.

By His agony and bloody sweat
  My soul from sin is free ;
I am secure from Satan's net,
  All from Calvary's tree.

Isaiah's prophecy was fulfill'd
  That Christ should die for all,
When by centurion his blood was spilled,
  And He aloud to God did call.

No scepticism can e'er control
    Or shake my trust in Thee.
By Thy Son's death we are made whole,
    And by faith and works we're free.

Glory to Father and to Son,
    For the sacrifices given
The seal of salvation is now done
    Which secures the pass to Heaven.

HYMN.

Thy bounties, Lord, are freely given,
    Our happiness to secure ;
Thou lookest down from Thy good Heaven,
    And tryest to make us pure.

Born in sin, but by Christ's blood,
    We're renewed and sanctified ;
For His enemies' malice He withstood
    As crucified He slowly died.

Thy goodness endureth to the end,
    To all here who it deserve ;
Thou dost to us great blessings send
    When we Thy word observe !

Thou watchest infancy's career
   In all its fickle ways ;
Maternal instincts Thou dost cheer,
   When Thou sendest love-lit rays.

And when to manhood's noble state
   · Thou presentest Thy holy law,
The high and low of whate'er fate,
   In Thy precepts find no flaw.

Pure and holy is Thy goodly plan,
   Thy promises are ne'er in vain,
For Thou saidst in Thy original plan
   That the good shall Heaven attain.

HYMN.

We cannot cheat Thee, Lord above,
   Though we may constant try ;
If in deceit our hearts are wove,
   Thou knowest the sinful lie.

When darkness draws a shadowy veil,
   We hope Thou wilt not spy ;
Yet the inward monitor tells the tale,
   In fear Thou shouldst be nigh.

We cheat ourselves in deceiving Thee,
   Though subtle be the act;
And if we accept a sinful fee,
   Thou knowest every fact.

Thy omniscient eye is o'er all,
   No matter where we be;
In humble cot or stately hall,
   Thine eye canst always see.

What fools we are to spend our time
   In trying Thee to defraud;
We'll never reach Thy happy clime
   Unless truth guides us on the road.

Lord, turn our hearts from lying sin;
   Give us both strength and grace,
That we Thy kingdom enter in
   When endeth this life's race.

HYMN.

When David wrote his songs of old,
   Inspired by good God above,
He prayed for wisdom more than gold,
   And asked Him for His love.

He put his confidence in Thee,
  O good Lord of Paradise,
And showed his great integrity,
  And heart so free from vice.

He prayed his enemies to forgive
  As Thou hadst him forgiven,
And asked that Thou his soul receive
  Into the realms of Heaven.

And so now, O God, thy children here
  Ask Thee, as David sought,
That Thou wouldst dry each pearly tear,
  For Christ our salvation wrought.

And when we leave this earthly scene
  And our bodies are laid low,
On Thee all our hopes now lean,
  That we shall hear Thy trumpet blow.

HYMN.

(FOR A CHILD).

O God, my mother taught me oft
  To say my prayers to You,
And now I cast my eyes aloft,
  A blessing for to sue.

I ask you to make me very good,
   And my kind mother e'er obey,
I trust you as Noah did in the flood
   When the ark drifted far away.

I wish you, Lord, now good-night,
   As I retire to my rest,
For I know that when I do aright
   'Tis then you love me best.

When I die, O will you take
   My soul up to sweet Heaven,
For mother said, for Jesus' sake,
   My sins will be forgiven.

HYMN.

BETHEL.

LORD, when high waves dash o'er the ship,
   And raging is the billowy sea,
When yard-arms in the ocean dip,
   'Tis then, O God, we trust to thee.

When scudding close-reef'd before the sea,
   And murky is the lowering sky,
And heavily rolling to the lee,
   We feel that Thou art ever nigh.

When the fore-mast goes by the board,
   And lee-rail under, we roll along,
The storm-sail strains its every cord,
   Yet still we sing our cheerful song.

For we're sustain'd by Thee, great God,
   Who makes the stormy winds to rise,
And canst calm them with Thy holy nod,
   From Thy haven beyond the skies.

And when we're bounding with fine breeze
   With every stitch of canvas spread,
When curling are the crested seas,
   We know Thou'rt looking out ahead.

And if close haul'd with tighten'd sheet,
   And steering closely to wind's eye,
As we to windward fain would beat,
   With a heavy list to leeward we lie.

And in midnight watch with every stitch
   Of sail set aloft, from stem to stern,
With majestic grace the ship will pitch,
   'Tis then to Thee our hearts will turn.

THE END.